To SUE,

2/1/14

Sekunjalo

(It has happened)

Gil Jackman

EDWARD GASKELL *publishers*
Cranford House
6 Grenville Street
Bideford
Devon
EX39 2EA

ISBN 1 -898546 -19 -3

Sekunjalo

(It has happened)

Typeset, Printed, and Bound by
The Lazarus Press
6 Grenville Street • Bideford
Devon • England • EX39 2EA

The Little Black Boy

My mother bore me in the southern wild,
And I am black, but O my soul is white;
White as an angel is the English child,
But I am black, as if bereaved of light.
My mother taught me underneath a tree,
And, sitting down before the heat of day,
She took me on her lap and kissed me,
And, pointing to the east, began to say:
'Look on the rising sun – there God does live,
And gives his light, and gives his heat away;
And flowers and trees and beasts and men receive
Comfort in morning, joy in the noonday.
And we are put on earth a little space,
That we may learn to bear the beams of love;
And these black bodies and this sunburnt face
Is but a cloud, and like a shady grove.
For when our souls have learned the heat to bear,
The cloud will vanish, we shall hear his voice
saying: "Come out from the grove, my love and care, And
round my golden tent like lambs rejoice"
Thus did my mother say, and kissed me;
And thus I say to little English boy.
When I from black, and he from white cloud free,
And round the tent of God like lambs we joy,
I'll shade him from the heat, till he can bear
To lean in joy upon our Father's knee;
And then I'll stand and stroke his silver hair,
And be like him, and he will then love me.

William Blake.

One

'You're the only one who could do the job, Phillip, and the only one I'd trust to do it,' he said. I could have preened at that, almost did in fact, before realising who I was talking with. 'Your television work has been excellent and you've proved your ability to get inside the obvious facts, but you've always had censorship from above. *White* censorship from above, Phillip. You still handled your subject matter in a manner I'm very impressed with, of course. But I've based my selection upon your books. There you had no censorship to contend with and you were allowed the freedom to address the issues correctly.'

Of course I had no censorship, you pretentious prick. *You* were the one who chose the subject matter in the first place, *You* gave me the format, *You* edited it, and *You* were the one who published it. The soul of black Britain, the man behind the ebony throne. Shit-stirrer in chief – Neville Ndongo. You pompous sod.

Despite a cynicism that had been my saving grace, I was still a pompous sod myself.

'Thank you, Neville. I'm grateful for your confidence.'

'Absolutely earned, my dear chap.' He spoke with a larger plum than any of my public school contemporaries, most of whom he would have put to shame in a debating society. Neville (two L's and an E) had begun life in the depths of Upper Parliament Street, the son of a labourer at Cammel Lairds. Before they'd started laying off, his father had worked overtime every night and all day Saturday to support a large family of five boys and three girls. They in turn supported the youngest – Neville – through college and on to university. He was a brilliant scholar, and could have gone to Oxbridge, but instead he chose the LSE, the infamous London School of Economics. Supporters of reds, lefties, Black Power, the IRA, Tariq Ali, Red Ken... and the rest. He studied economics, sociology, and Marxism – though not the Marxism of Karl the founder. Because of his blackness, not despite it as the popular press might misquote, he began to espouse the cause of the melanin-enriched citizens of our green and pleasant land. Which leads me to side-track slightly here in the cause of political correctness, which of course is applicable to minority groups, but I must confess largely originates from racial dissatisfaction.

If we can't say 'black', then it follows that 'white' is equally verboten. As in the fairy story, 'Snow Melanin-Impoverished and the Seven Vertically-Challenged Individuals'. What a panto that would make. Where was I? Neville. I lie not about his brilliance; the man holds a doctorate in social sciences, (easy enough, he sneered), and an LLB so he can defend the scum out there. Don't get me wrong, I think the world of Neville, and respect what he stands for. Or did. He just gets up my nose at times. Most times, in fact. He's dedicated his life to the black cause, but he's as much a product of racism as anyone who lives behind a barrier of their own colour. I'm black too, so what does that make me? A question I've asked Neville many times, though I've never had a satisfactory answer. While he was studying at the LSE, he took part in amateur dramatics, of which elocution lessons were an integral part. Neville of course went to extremes, and now he makes Trevor McDonald sound ethnic, and Sloanes think they have speech impediments.

'I'm still not quite clear what you want me to do, Neville,' I said apologetically. I was very apologetic back then. Before the Africa thing.

'I haven't been very precise, have I?' He had a way of smiling and trying to be humble at the same time that made you want to apologise instead. It was something which really incompetent cabinet ministers do very well, safe in what they erroneously thought was the sanctity of their office.

'No, you haven't,' I agreed, with the forthrightness of familiarity. Neville was some ten years older than me, but I remembered him from years ago, when he was plain Billy Jamieson. Where the Ndongo came from no-one knew, for he was as indigenous as I was. His people and mine were landed together on the Liverpool wharf around 1807, when slavery was abolished. Hundreds of African blacks were rescued by the Royal Navy, and dumped on one of the five docks that existed then. The Old Dock, St Georges, Salt House, and the King's and Queen's Docks. They were not returned to the shores of Africa, nor could they have described where they came from if the offer had been made. So they assimilated with the locals. After a fashion. Mating would perhaps have been a rather romantic way of describing the merging of two alien cultures. Rutting might have been more accurate, for over the next few centuries the black African – like the Irishman – became part of the Scouse culture.

Neville was offering me a job. Getting to the point with Neville is never the easiest thing. First he calls in all the cards, like favours owed, favours due, favours yet to be asked; and then he hits on compatible skin. I began to realise that *Africa* was the destination, and I began to feel... peculiar.

Where *was* Africa? or rather, *Afrika*. Was freedom *Uhuru*, *Inkululeko* or *Amandhla*? And did it matter anyway?

'We want the truth, that is all, Phillip,' Neville was

saying. 'Simply the truth. And we will publish it. You can rest assured, my friend.'

'Yes, thank you, Neville,' I said, exasperation in my voice. 'Perhaps a few more details could be allowed to escape you?'

'Of course,' he said, in the manner of an affronted country squire. 'We are appointing you to go to South Africa and give us the *true* story of what's happening out there. Are our people all right?'

'Our people?' What the hell was he talking about? There were times I had the feeling that a broom closet had more depth than Neville.

'Of course... the African people,' he frowned. 'The heritage that we both stem from, Phillip. Never forget your heritage. It's what we are here for, after all.'

'Neville,' I hissed patiently, if such a thing is possible. 'What exactly do you want? I've given up my television career to write. Now you want me to give up that to become a journeyman for the black press.'

'Not at all,' he sniffed. 'I'm asking you to commit.' He said it as though it was a nasty word.

'Commit? I've always committed,' I said. 'Don't give me that crap, Neville. I'm as committed as you are.' Neville worked out of a set of dingy offices off Oxford Street. The building was clean and well maintained so the landlord could charge exorbitant rents. On the other hand, Neville's offices were purposefully dingy so he could qualify for the many grants he applied for under the auspices of his Afro-Asian press. The only Asian influence was a plateful of take-away samoosas I'd seen there once.

Not many people were aware that Neville himself was the landlord, for he owned the freehold on the entire block.

'Journalists from all over the world are descending on Southern Africa prior to the elections next year. They are sending back reports about the last days of apartheid, in all its naked vulgarity.'

I nearly asked him about the naked vulgarity of

the treatment of the Aborigine, or the black man in the southern states of America. Nearly, but didn't. I liked the sound of what he was leading up to.

'We want to be the first to publish a book about it all. The degradation that our people had to suffer under the apartheid system. The beatings, the tortures, the murders carried out by the Police. We don't want a cover-up, or a white-wash, if you'll pardon the pun. In the spirit of peace and harmony there is going to be a lot of that, Phillip. We want a completely honest and subjective view of the last days of the white Nationalist Government, that has held total power for 45 years.' Neville leaned back in his chair and rubbed his hands over his eyes. I'd never really noticed how small his hands were. 'You have proved your integrity twice now in your books, Phillip, and I want you to do it again. I want a book completed by the end of next February, then we add a final chapter after the election itself and get it out to the retailers. The big chains will love it. The black people will love it,' he added quickly. He placed his elbows on the cluttered desk before him, cupping his chin in his hands and frowning. Neville was a creature of body language, and I knew him well enough to realise that money was about to be introduced into the conversation.

'I won't deny we've just completed a very good year, Phillip,' he admitted. 'But as you know, I've never been a believer in massive payments up front. I can offer you a good advance and your expenses. Both will come out of eventual sales, of course.'

'Of course,' I murmured, aware of Neville's interpretation of 'good' when it came to an advance.

'You like the idea, then?'

'Very much, Neville,' I replied. Of course, the old fraud was gambling on the success of the Publishers' Prize, and was afraid someone else might get in with a commission if he didn't. I'd have done it for the expenses alone, of course, but he didn't know that. Then he said something that emptied my mind of such unworthy

9

thoughts as to his black fanaticism and legendary meanness.

'I'm offering you an advance of fifty thousand pounds,' he said.

'Fifty thou...' I repeated when my heart started up again. 'Who do you want me to kill, Neville?'

It was said as a joke, but by the look in his eyes I don't think he found it funny.

'No-one,' he replied, and his voice seemed to come from far away. 'The killing has already been done. Would you like a drink, Phillip?'

I nodded, surprised at the offer. All the time I'd known him, from the early days of his tiny squalid office off Upper Parliament Street, through the years I'd been coming down to London, I'd never known him drink during the day. He took out a bottle of Tullymore Dew from his desk, a traditional brew from our visits to the Irish clubs in Liverpool. It was already half empty. He poured generous tots into two coffee mugs and we toasted each other. He drank his off and poured another.

The drink seemed to put some fire back into him, and he gave me a steady look. 'Do you remember John Barnes? I introduced you last year. He worked for our magazine, SABLE.'

'Yes,' I nodded. 'Nice looking young man. I think I made some remarks about football, with his having the same name as Liverpool's striker. Reporter, wasn't he?'

Neville nodded. The faraway look had come back to his eyes. 'He was a very good reporter. Like yourself he believed in digging deeply for the truth. He'd get to the bottom of any story that came along, no matter how he felt personally about it. Which is why they murdered him.'

I sat stunned for a few moments. I'd read SABLE of course, like any black person in Britain who wished to be informed on matters pertinent to the race. Some disturbing news came from its pages, and to give the editor his due, not all stories were pro-black or anti-white. Neville was that editor, and the circulation was such that it had made him a wealthy man. Not that he would ever admit to it.

'Who murdered him,' I asked finally, 'and why?'

'Those two questions are what I want *you* to answer, my friend,' Neville said, and I was shocked to see tears welling up in his eyes. I looked away, embarrassed. 'Your cover story is genuine and a book should come from it, but it is not the main reason you're going. I want to know who, and I want to know why. John was a gentle creature, but he would delve into a story long after it was prudent to do so. I want you to be very careful out there, Phillip. If you still choose to go.'

I nodded slowly. 'Tell me what happened to John Barnes.'

Two

In the innocent days of our youth, while we strive for recognition as adults, memorable incidents occur which shape our later lives. They form influences that direct our future and they can be beneficial, or not, depending upon our perceptions at that time. I was nine when I first saw Martin Luther King on the television. My father was a doctor so we were among the privileged few of Liverpool to own a television set in 1963. It was the 28th August and the occasion was Washington's largest demonstration to date. Over 200,000 people, not only black but also whites in their thousands, demanding civil rights for black people. This came a century after a man called Lincoln had taken his nation to bloody war for those same black rights. And supposedly won. When Martin Luther King began 'I have a dream...' I became absorbed, totally immersed in his words. The peaceful struggle he advocated impressed me immeasurably. Even at nine years of age.

Five years later, when the man of non-violent resistance met his violent end, like his hero Gandhi, I was devastated. Life wasn't fair. But didn't I always know that?

A couple of years after King died I read about a black man in Alabama who was savagely beaten, castrated, then burned to death by a mob of whites. A 73 year old white woman had been raped and chopped to pieces with a garden spade. Local opinion was that only a nigger would rape a 73 year old woman, and the fact that he was her gardener was proof positive. Ergo; burn the nigger. No-one was ever charged with the man's murder, and the investigation closed after forty-eight hours. A week later they caught an escapee from a nearby mental institution, who confessed to the rape killing. He provided details that only the murderer could have known. He was white. The last incident happened while I was waiting to go to university. My father read something from the newspaper he usually hid behind. It was not like him, for breakfast was his quiet time of the day, prior to spending long hours at his surgery, then innumerable house calls. It was a lengthy article that dealt with the Republic of South Africa and the repulsiveness of the apartheid system. We were all suitably subdued by his eloquent reading, not least by the content. My sister was impressed enough to join the British anti-apartheid movement the next day. I was simply impressed; though I'm sure that's not the best word to use for such a subject. In 1993 I won the United Kingdom Publishers' Prize with my second work of non-fiction. Not that I'd ever written a work of fiction, considering it a degrading form of literature to travel that path of easy money. Writing about people who don't exist, in places that do, but are thinly disguised as somewhere else. These were my disdainful thoughts at that time. *Liverpool : Founded on Sin* told how the prosperity and greatness of the famous port had been derived from two activities which would today be regarded as criminal in the extreme. Slavery and privateering. Liverpool's coat-of-arms bears the motto *Deus nobis haec otia fecit* literally translated as *God has given all these things to us*. Not strictly true, however, for the riches of the great ports, including Bristol and London, were not God-given as claimed. They simply helped themselves.

Privateering was a licensed form of piracy, being a

by-product of war. They held the sovereign's commission and blessing for a successful voyage, with the said sovereign naturally expecting a goodly share of the profits. The privateers' motives were ninety-nine per cent greed to one part true patriotism.

The nefarious slave trade could find not even a one per cent excuse for its actions. The seeds of the racial problems of the world today were sown in those early days of the 18th century by a handful of profit-seeking Liverpool merchants. A sweeping statement? Perhaps. But why pick on Liverpool? No one reason in particular. I happened to be born there, knew it well; and it seemed a good idea at the time. Also, I'd once made a documentary for Anglia television about slavery in general so had most of the research material at my fingertips. My first book *Black Identity in the United Kingdom*, had been about the plight of Afro-Caribbeans in Britain; rapidly losing their cultural identities to the predominantly white society they were drawn into. British pubs, British theatre, British culture; all-absorbing and all-powerful, slowly stealing their wild Afro-Caribbean souls.

It was very successful and brought much acclaim from the black community. Not only at home but from across the Atlantic too. The African-American society gave it the Black Heritage Award, 'for the furtherance of ethnic roots in an alien environment'. Ironically, both books were successful not because of what they contained, but for what they did not.

For 2000 years people from other lands have settled in the Isles of Britain, merging and integrating with the indigenous population. It began with Julius Caesar about 37BC, and he had his hands full with the little Celtic cross-dressers, some of whom had a strange penchant for blue makeup. Claudius finally subdued Britain and the Romans hung around for another 400 years – roughly, a timespan equal to that from just before the crowning of James 1 of England until the present day. Many legions eventually consisted of

Britons born under Roman occupation who considered themselves Roman citizens – and were proud of it.

When the Romans did leave, a dark age descended upon the land with only the occasional glimmer of light reflecting the bitter struggles of Vortigern, Uther Pendragon, King Arthur and the infant Christian church against the formidable fighting men of Norway Sweden and Denmark. Norsemen raped and pillaged, with some staying on to till the soil and breed.

King Alfred, and ultimately King Harold stood their ground before finally succumbing to the irre-sistable might and organisation of the French-Norman King William – The Conqueror. His cousins and friends flooded across the channel and divided Britain between them. They have owned it ever since.

During the next millenium battered survivors of an Armada were washed up around the coasts as their ships fled from the wrath of Drake's seamen. Refugees from Europe, seeking sanctuary from two world wars limped across the channel seeking a more peaceful life; and even German prisoners-of-war found wives and a new life among their former foes. Asians too – following the Partition of India – showed little faith in a country ran by their own leaders, and used the last gift of the Imperialists – British passports

Then came the influx of the blacks. Ghana, Nigeria, Kenya, Jamaica, Trinidad, Barbados; from everywhere in Africa and the Caribbean. Like those before them they came to the shores of Britain for a bet-ter life; a different life. Now they claimed loss of their own ethos, for they did not want a *different* life, but a *better* one in the same culture and surroundings they'd left, so now they tried to change the new country in which they were guests.

And what of the other black people of Britain? The ones who had been here for three centuries already, and spoke with the local dialects of Birmingham and Manchester, Wales and Scotland, London and Bristol;

and Liverpool, where the black invasion had first began.

Why then should the latest arrivals to the tiny isles be given preference over anyone else? Why should Britain have to accept cannabis-smoking Rastafarianism as a religion? And give tax-payers' money away in so-called 'cultural' grants? For that matter who do the Muslims think they are to set up their own parliament? Or to put a fatwa on Salman Rushdie. Personally I can't stand the man, making snide remarks about royalty from the safety of his £1 million round-the-clock protection, paid for by that same over-burdened tax-payer. Every time I see his smug bewhiskered arrogance peering from the pages of a newspaper I get angry. I'd even impugn his writing, to the extent that the great reading public at large would probably never have heard of him if it hadn't been for the sympathy aroused by the fiendish Muslims, who are actually his own people, after all. But that might be construed as jealousy.

These thoughts are with me now, as I know they were then. I was aware of the inconsistencies in my writing, but did not allow myself to dwell on them at that time. It was not what people wanted to hear. I had majored in sociology, and history was an ingredient of that discipline, so I could not profess ignorance. I well understood the motives and customs of those early Englishmen, and to do so one had to take into account the narrow world in which they lived at that time. High infant mortality and a short expectation of adult life made everyone exist in close proximity to death. Religion was the opiate of the masses before Marx ever wrote it down as a profound revelation, and the fear of hell and damnation for the wicked was a very real thing.

The Bible was interpreted (or misinterpreted) in myriad ways. The Commandment 'Love thy neighbour' did not include the savage heathen, for he could hardly be considered a neighbour. His purpose on the earth could only be as slave to the white man, for his status was that of an animal, and as he could not be reasoned with he had to be trained like one. Fear of pain was the only expedient way to ensure obedience. He was chained to prevent escape, but if he did so he was hunted down and flogged. He was branded on the forehead in case he was captured by another slave owner.

But slavery was right. Was it not laid down in the Bible, and supported by the clergy of the time? The Rev John Newton, later Rector of St Mary's, a friend of Cowper, and author of the Olney hymns, was a slaver Captain while he studied for the ministry.

Politicians also favoured the slave trade, and the speeches made by both parties in the Parliamentary Election of 1761 were unanimously in favour of free trade to Africa, with no restrictions on slavery. It was widely agreed that blacks were an inferior race; to be bought and sold by the white man, with his brand upon them.

Not everyone saw it as such. To quote a Liverpool writer of 1884: 'It was a traffic so vile, so replete with the worst of crimes, it was the blackest stain on poor humanity, and I cannot find words to fully express my abhorrence of the traffic...'

These, then, were the mitigating facts, (slight as they might appear), omitted from my much admired text. Not that my awareness made any difference over the greater fact that black people wanted to know the full weight of the sins against them, with no liberty of excuse for cause and effect.

Just as they would not be interested in knowing that the British seamen of the day did not have to go ashore and raid native villages to obtain their cargoes of black ivory. They had no need. The local chiefs were only too happy to round up their own people in exchange for brightly coloured cloths from the mills of Lancashire, a few handfuls of sparkling beads, and some axe heads.

Even the Booker Prize began to get involved with my humble effort, despite the fact that it was widely described as a definitive work of non-fiction. 'So was

Schindler's Ark,' a member of the so-called literati proclaimed, but the saner members of the judging panel held out.

I have to confess that I was 'far enough up myself', as they say in Liverpool, to actually feel gratified at the proposed selection. Not only was the book regarded as 'revealing', and 'essential reading', but it was now accepted as 'literature' which pleased me immensely.

Until later, when a tell-it-as-it-is literary critic, who by some freak of divine mis-matching was also a friend, told me why. That year they had no large list of unknown, unheard of, (and largely unreadable), foreigners with unpronounceable names, and were getting embarrassed that it might have to go to, heaven forbid, a white Englishman. Which was where I came in.

As I said before, despite the lyrical name of Phillip Christie O'Brien and a public school education, I was as black as Neville. Which made me a worthy candidate in the primary selections.

Three

'The purpose of your visit, *meneer*?' The customs man asked the question politely enough, but there was something in his manner that I found offensive. It was something I couldn't quite put my finger on, yet I would come across it often during my time in South Africa.

'Pleasure mainly,' I replied with an equanimity I didn't feel at the time. 'I'm also collecting material for a book.'

'Pleasure,' he repeated, and looked sideways at his companion. 'And you're going to write a book, eh?' He spoke as he might if I'd told him I was about to turn his desk into solid gold.

'Yes, it will be my third one,' I said too loudly. For some reason I wanted this supercilious bastard to know exactly who I was, and what I'd done.

'We're very impressed,' his colleague spoke for the first time. He was older, and his accent was far more pronounced, the harsh vowel sounds grating on the ear.

One had to remember that English was their second language here in the Transvaal, but I'd often heard that accent on the news. Usually when a huge Afrikaner policeman was being interviewed following the breakup of a crowd with bullets and tear gas.

I had visions of a cold, lonely cell with some poor black man lying broken and bleeding in a corner, as the door slammed shut on half a dozen cops with clubs and whips.

'Enjoy your stay, *meneer*,' the younger one handed my passport back. Just like that. No baggage search. I could go. As I hefted my suitcase off the counter and began to walk towards the doorway marked exit, I heard a chuckle behind me.

'What were you expecting? To be beaten with a *sjambok* and called *kaffir*?' I turned and looked up at the man who'd been sitting across the aisle on the plane. I say looked up because he was extremely tall, and I'm not exactly a midget myself at 5' 11". We'd exchanged a few pleasantries during the long journey, and I'd learned he was an American journalist working for a cable news agency. He was also the blackest man I'd ever clapped eyes on. I'd never seen such depth of colour – or rather lack of it. He was pitch-black, coal-black, jet-black, inky-black; every adjective you can imagine. The 'cyprus black as e'er was crow' of Shakespeare. He was also handsome, with features that were regular in the Caucasian way, aquiline almost. Unlike mine. I owe more to Eddie Murphy than Harry Belafonte, thanks to a nose that was my main defence when gaining my boxing blue.

'I didn't know quite what to expect,' I said with self-conscious huffiness, then smiled when I saw his eyebrows arch. 'Yes, I suppose I was expecting something other than politeness, and I don't wish to appear ungrateful, but I still sensed something behind the facade.'

'You're right,' he fell into step beside me, and made an obvious effort to come down to my pace. 'Ten years ago they would have given you a hard time, gone through everything and tossed your gear around, but this is the 'New Africa' and people have to be very careful not to offend. Especially the whiteys.'

I frowned slightly but did not ask the obvious question. We had now emerged into the spacious twin level terminal of Jan Smuts Airport. Something like five million passengers used the airport each year, and it looked like they were all due in at the same time, judging by the crowds of families and friends waiting in the main hall.

'Is anyone meeting you?' my companion asked, and when I shook my head I received the arched eyebrows again. 'Well, Jo'burg is a good forty-five minutes from here, and I don't fancy your chances of catching a cab or a courtesy bus. Can I give you a lift?'

'Well, I...'

'Good, that's settled then,' he took my arm and led me across to the Imperial Car Hire desk. 'I've a car booked. These people took over from Hertz when they pulled out of South Africa. Their loss, if you ask me. By the way, the name's Jackson, Tom. And no relation to Jesse or Michael, so don't ask.'

The girls on the desk were both charming and efficient and we were loaded up and on our way in no time at all. It was a BMW 500i, and I remarked that he must be on a good expense account to afford such a top echelon car.

'It might be top echelon in the UK,' he smiled. 'But out here BMWs and Mercedes are wall to wall. The white farmers wouldn't be seen dead without their big Mercs and 4 x 4s.'

He was just explaining that a 4 x 4 was a twin cab *bakkie*, and that a *bakkie* was a four-wheel drive flat top, when a bright red 7-Series Mercedes went past with a fat black man at the wheel.

Tom laughed at my expression. 'No, he ain't the chauffeur. Chauffeurs don't smoke $20 cigars. Not when they're driving, at any rate. The man *owns* the wheels, Phil baby.'

I was too surprised to argue over the diminutive of my name. 'But how did...?'

'My friend, there are a lot of very rich black folks in this country. Just as there are a lot of poor white folks. The papers make it sound like there's never been poor whites before, which is crap. Eighty years ago this country had a poor white problem, and *apartheid* was considered the best way of solving it. Scrapping *apartheid* gave them poor whites again.'

He glanced at me out of the corner of his eye. 'How much reading did you do on this place before you left Limeyville?'

'Not a lot,' I smiled. 'Mainly the geography, but that was deliberate. I wanted to gain my impressions at first hand, not what someone else had written with their own bias and prejudice.'

'Right,' he said carefully. 'And you one dude dat don't got none of neither, huh?'

I found his habit of lapsing into street jive disconcerting, and I gazed out of the window before replying. We were on a three lane motorway, passing through suburbs of houses and industrial estates, with none of the wonderful countryside I'd expected.

'I'm sure I have,' I admitted finally. 'Like most people bias and prejudice begin with the colour of your skin, takes in your experiences of life, and is inevitably decided by what remains in your heart afterwards.'

'Sounds good, Phil, especially when you say it in that BBC voice of yours,' he said drily. 'I must tell you I've read both your books, by the way.'

He didn't elaborate. Not then.

'This place is getting into a reverse racism situation at the moment. Blacks are being shunted up the management ladder, and whites are losing their jobs. Retrenchment they call it. I'm not saying it ain't before time; the black people in this country have been held back for too long. Lack of education has resulted in poor job opportunities etcetera, etcetera. But it now leaves a situation where people are getting jobs because of the colour of their skin, *not* their ability to do those jobs.'

'But what about before?' I retorted. 'The whites had a monopoly on work *and* education. What chance did a black man have of getting the qualifications for useful employment?'

'True in the main, but there was always *some* opportunity. Don't forget there have been black lawyers and doctors around for a long time. Ghandi, that old guy in the diapers, got his law degree from here, remember?'

'I suppose you're right to some extent,' I conceded. 'After all, Nelson Mandela was a lawyer.'

'Not before he went to Club Med for 27 years he wasn't,' the journalist grinned. 'He was a murderer, a terrorist – or a freedom fighter; whichever you prefer. What he *wasn't* was a lawyer. He did a correspondence course while he was on Robben Island, my man.'

'What about his doctorate?' I protested.

'What doctorate?' Tom snorted. 'After his release he had a half dozen *honorary* doctorates heaped on him, but he's never qualified for one. No more than Buthelezi has. The man went to Oxford but didn't pass diddly-squat. Finally got a BA from Fort Hare. At least old Nelson doesn't call himself "Doctor" like Buthelezi does.'

'Maybe that's the media's fault, not his. Just whose side are you on, Tom?'

'Side? I ain't on anyone's side, bro... Sheeét!' He cursed suddenly as a car overtook on the inside and whipped in front of us. Passing on the inside is allowed in SA, a practice that scared the crap out of me, as my American friend would say. 'Where was I? Oh, yeah. No, I ain't on no-one's side but my own, *and* the millions of people out there that pay to hear the news. I mean the *real* news – not what the policy-makers and jerk-offs want to hear – but THE TRUTH, in capital letters.'

Like Neville, TRUTH in capitals.

'Christ,' I said in wonder. 'I do believe you mean it.'

'Sure I mean it. You can bet your black ass on that,' he grinned, and pointed ahead. 'Now, we are just entering *Egoli* – the place of gold – as the Zulus call

Jo'burg. SA produces more gold than any other country on earth, and this is where it all began in 1886. Over to the west of the city is the George Harrison Park, which is *not* named after your Beatle townie, but an Aussie who found gold on the Witwatersrand reef. He pegged the first claim – sold it for £10 – and vanished for ever.'

I sat in silence as the enormity of it sank in. The man who could have been the richest human being of all time simply took ten quid and disappeared.

High-rise buildings had sprung up around us, and the architecture seemed to be based more on height than beauty of design. I mentioned this to Tom Jackson.

'Yeah, this place seems to change every year,' he nodded. 'Any building over 20 years old is only standing because the property developers haven't gotten around to it yet.'

We were now driving along one of the main roads into the centre of the city, and I saw it was signposted Rissik Street. The width of the streets helped to allay the feeling of being hemmed in by the towering blocks on either side.

'Just over a hundred years since it was a shanty town, and now Jo'burg is the largest mining, manufacturing and engineering centre in Africa,' he sounded like a tour guide. 'It's crawled through grubby infancy, hole-in-the-pants adolescence, and brawling youth; and now it's settled down to sober, middle-aged respectability.'

'Wow,' I said sarcastically. 'You sound like a journalist.'

'I should do,' he laughed. 'That's a quote from the first piece I ever did on this town. Now, pal, where do you want to go? I'm borrowing a pad from a guy I know, and you're welcome to share. For a week, at least, then I'm off to Durban. What d'you say?'

I accepted.

Tom's friend was a South African colleague working in Washington, Tom's home town, for a year, and judging by his flat he was either an extremely hard-working and successful journalist, or his parents were very rich.

'His parents are very rich,' Tom grinned when I asked. The flat was in Hillbrow, a cosmopolitan community lying on the top of Hospital Hill ridge, and it had two distinctions. It was the most densely populated residential area in Southern Africa; and it was dominated by the tallest building in the whole of Africa – the 269 metre high Strijdom Tower.

I'd liked Tom Jackson on sight, and the more I got to know him the better that liking became. His background was not unlike Neville's, in that his father had carried a menial job for his whole life with the sole ambition of getting his only son through college. This Tom had achieved, and made his father proud of him with a degree in journalism. There the resemblance ended. Neville fervently espoused the black cause while posturing as a white with his over-accentuated speech and foppy dressing – I'd often wondered if he was gay – while Tom, on the other hand, fervently believed in the truth, no matter if it came down on the side of black or white, and showed a naivety in his pride of being an American that belied the colour of his skin.

'In my book there are no Afro-Americans, Native-Americans or Eurocentric-Americans,' he declared that first night, as we attacked a huge jug of Margaritas he'd made. 'Next we'll be talking about Canine-Americans instead of fucking dogs. That thing makes for racism, man. Look, I only know you're a Limey by the way you talk – which is how most of us identify. That guy Bruno, the boxer? Now he talks like that other Limey with the good left hook that decked Cassius that time.... Right, Henry Cooper. So what's the difference? Their skins ain't the same, so what? They're the same kind of guys, right?'

He *was* right, and we were getting drunk, but there was nothing wrong with that. I was getting an education, and after all, any education pertaining to

South Africa could only be useful to me in my quest for the truth about John Barnes.

I began to tell the journalist the main reason I was there. He sat up straighter in his chair and appeared more sober as I talked.

'They found him just off the N12 outside Pot...che...stom...' I floundered with the Afrikaans.

'Potchefstroom,' Tom supplied.

'His head, fingers and genitals had been cut off,' I tried to shock him. 'They were never found.'

Instead of being shocked he said only one word. It sounded like 'mooti'. When I queried it he shook his head.

'The official report claimed it was a *tribal killing*,' I carried on. 'John Barnes was born in London. He was abandoned as a baby and brought up in an orphanage. He never knew his parents and had no links back to Africa. So how could they call it *tribal*?'

'Tribal as in "he was black",' Tom growled. 'To the cops out here we all belong to the black tribes of Africa, no matter where we come from. Call an Afrikaner a Dutchman and see how impressed he is.'

'But they *are* Dutchmen.'

'No they *ain't*, buddy....' he smiled without humour. 'Their ancestors might have come from the Netherlands, but they ain't Dutch. No more than you or I are African. You're English and I'm American. Back in July the House subcommittee on Census, Statistics and Postal Personnel met.' He poured the last of the Margaritas into our glasses. 'They met to see whether the present classification system should be changed for the next US census in the year 2000. In 1977 the Carter administration gave us five groups and definitions, but what about the people who are outside of these; half-castes maybe? It's mind boggling, man. Some poor guy came up with the unique idea of calling everyone multi-racial and he was shouted down by all the civil rights groups. Especially the black ones, who said that Directive 9 had "immeasurably assisted"

African-Americans. What we have there is a *neo-apartheid* system by the minorities.'

'Phew,' I shook my head in bewilderment. 'I didn't realise I'd asked a question.'

Tom began laughing at that, then I joined in and we were off for the next ten minutes. I tried to get the conversation back to the ill-fated John Barnes, but Tom crawled to his feet and shook his head.

'I'm turning in, Phil, I'm bushed,' he said. 'Tomorrow I'll take you to the main Police Station and you can do your enquiries, but I'll tell you now you're wasting your time. Then I'm going to show you Jo'burg. In a few days I'll take you to a pal of mine who will tell you a few things.'

He weaved his way to bed, although I got the impression he wasn't so drunk. I wandered over to the bookcase and took down a Zulu-English dictionary. After some difficulty I thought I'd found the word Tom had muttered, but it made no sense. Not then.

It was *Muti* – medicine.

I shrugged, and followed Tom's example by turning in.

Four

'Please be seated, *meneer*,' the grey-haired man said. He wore civilian clothes and had a beer gut that prevented his jacket closing properly. He did not offer to shake hands. 'I am Detective Warrant Officer van Zyl. How can I *help* you?'

His strong Afrikaner accent made it sound like *yelp*. I told him the purpose of my visit to SAP Headquarters in John Vorster Square. I understood he had been the officer who dealt with the case.

'That is correct,' he said carefully. 'The body was found at the beginning of June. It was put down as a tribal killing.'

'How could it be a tribal killing?' I asked, keeping my voice under control. 'He was English.'

'*Ja*, but 'e was blick,' he shrugged. 'As he had no head, how could we know 'e wasn't a S'African?'

'But when you *did* find out who he was,' I persisted. 'How could you still believe it to be tribal?'

He smiled thinly. 'The classification is made on any blick person who is killed in a violent way by persons who are believed to be non-white.' He said it parrot-fashion, as though reading from a book.

'How do you know it wasn't a white person who killed him?' I asked quietly. 'There are no black people out here who would have a reason to kill him. Why

28

didn't you...?'

'That's fuckin' enuff, *kaffir*.' It was there at last. That word. 'Don't tell me how to do my job. There's the door.'

I sat where I was. 'The file,' I said tightly.

'*What*?' He was standing now, and leaning over the desk in what he thought was a threatening manner.

'The investigation file. I would like to see it.'

His paunch was resting on the edge of the desk and I found this amusing. 'Are you smirkin' at me, *kaffir*?'

'No, Warrant Officer,' I said mildly. 'I'm actually laughing at the sight of your belly flowing all over the desk, and if you use that word on me again I'll make it flow somewhere else. In fact you'll be wearing it on your back as a hump.'

His face was a dark red, and where our conversation would have gone from there neither he nor I will ever know. I hadn't heard the door open, so was surprised when the voice came from behind me.

'Get out van Zyl, before you face another disciplinary board. And you will apologise to this gentleman before you go.'

A tall man came into my field of vision from the right. He was also wearing civvies, but a lot smarter than the man who began to move towards the door. He paused to mumble something at me and I waved a hand. It was more in dismissal than acknowledgement.

As the door closed the tall man beckoned me to be seated again and sat down behind the desk himself.

'I'm sorry about that, Mr O'Brien,' he said, his Afrikaans accent was much softer. 'I'm Major Strijdom. Van Zyl is a good policeman in many ways, but diplomacy is not one of his strong suits.'

I smiled at the understatement. 'His form of address leaves a lot to be desired, too.'

'Yes, Warrant Officer van Zyl could definitely be described as a racist,' he said frankly. 'We're not all like that, I assure you. I assume you know what the word means, Mr O'Brien?'

I frowned. 'It means nigger, or wog, doesn't it?'

'Not at all,' he smiled. 'It actually comes from the Arabic, which simply means *unbeliever*. Now, I believe you're enquiring about the John Barnes case?'

'Yes, and if it's possible I'd like to have a look at the file – or at least the pathologist's report.'

'I'm afraid that's not possible,' he said and gave me a rather strange look. 'Are you a relative of the deceased?'

'No,' I replied. 'I understand he had no relatives. I'm representing his editor, and met him only once. Would that make any difference to my seeing the file?'

'No, not at all,' he said. 'It's simply not possible, relative or otherwise.'

'Your warrant officer said it was a tribal killing, but he wouldn't elaborate. What does that mean, Major? And how did you identify the body without fingerprints, or a head?'

'By the mutilations, Mr O'Brien, it appeared to be ritualistic, which we class under tribal.' He shrugged. 'Certain body parts were removed and carried away, showing that was what they wanted and the reason he was killed. As for identification, we'd received missing person reports from his hotel and employer mentioning certain scars, and a small tattoo.'

He stood up and extended a hand and I realised the interview was over, unrewarding and unsatisfactory as it may have been.

I repeated the details of the visit to Tom, who made no comment. The rest of the week went by quickly. Tom did no work other than a few phone calls, and took it upon himself to be my guide and mentor. We took in the art gallery in Joubert Park, which housed works by English, French and Dutch masters. We attended a concert by the National Symphony Orchestra domiciled in the city, and Tom insisted we visit the extensive zoo in the Hermann Eckstein Park.

'Apart from the game farms and reserves, there

ain't no live ones roaming around out there no more,' he said, and I detected a note of sadness in his voice. We watched rugby at Ellis Park; cricket at the Wanderers' ground; and soccer at the Rand Stadium – despite my insistence that I didn't care for any of those sports.

The nightlife was Tom's speciality, and we went to risque reviews and clubs until the early hours of the morning. Nowhere did we meet open opposition or racism, and there were as many black faces among the clientele as white.

Towards the end of the week I was woken early in the morning by my host, bearing a cup of coffee and the news that we were leaving in fifteen minutes.

'Now that you've seen the civilised side of the Transvaal,' he watched with amusement as I stumbled from shower to shaving mirror and finally into clothes, 'I'm going to show you the contrast, which is one of the reasons you came here in the first place – to see how the other half lives. *And* you will meet my friend.'

I must have frowned because he rose to his full height of 6' 6" and grinned. 'That's right, Phil baby. We're going to Soweto.'

Five

Johannesburg is pleasantly mild in summer, with the days warm to hot and the nights cool and refreshing. Most of the rain falls in summer, usually in the form of afternoon thunderstorms. These are sudden, brief, and often spectacular.

We hit one of the spectacular ones as we drove out to the township. As we left, the sky was filled with gigantic cloud castles of white cumulus, great dollops of whipped cream that floated lazily through the sky as though without purpose. Ten minutes later they'd turned black as tremendous electrical charges built up.

Then came the lightening. Most flashes are hidden in cloud, and I'd read in a local guide that modern buildings are normally unaffected by lightening, for conductors carry the discharge safely to earth. Motor vehicles were also unaffected according to the guide. I wondered where the conductors where on a car.

'Don't worry,' Tom grinned. 'The ground flashes are the only kind of lightening that cause damage.'

'Well, there seems to be enough of them,' I muttered.

'Yeah, about one in six hit the ground, but they only release their energy for one thousandth of a second.'

'Long enough to turn us both into charred embers.'

'Don't reckon it'd show on me too much,' he shrugged and I returned his grin. Somehow those violent flashes in the sky didn't seem so bad with the big American beside you. He inspired confidence.

We were now passing through the outskirts of Johannesburg, driving along streets without pavements, with row upon row of dingy houses on either side. Most had extra rooms attached, constructed from whatever was close to hand on the day building started. People leaning on fences or sitting on doorsteps broke off their conversation to stare at us.

'We seem to be getting black looks from the people out there,' I said straight faced.

'Sure,' he replied. 'Fancy car, couple of well-fed, well-dressed guys like us; what do you expect? We could be cops, bailiffs, government agents, union bosses, political recruiters. Any number of people bent on making their miserable lives worse.'

'In that case,' I said lightly, 'How come they haven't attacked us yet?'

'They might well do before the day's out.' There was no smile on his face. 'I'm taking you to visit a man named Chele Mopane. Nice guy. His place is right in the middle of this dump.'

'Thanks a lot,' I murmured.

'This is the largest of all the Black townships,' he said thoughtfully. 'The name itself is an acronym from the first two letters of *South Western Townships*,' he had a habit of talking as he would write. 'It's a city in itself, probably the fourth largest on the continent, and it grew out of the slums that resulted from thousands of Blacks flocking in from the rural areas in search of work before World War Two. Now it's reckoned there's around two million people here: Zulu, Xhosa, Venda, Sotho... you name it.'

He pointed to where a grey mound of buildings and chimneys, with tall pylons reaching to the sky, poked above the tiny rooftops. 'That's the power station at the Orlando East entrance. It supplies electricity to White Jo'burg, but all the Blacks get is the pollution from the coal smoke and the steam of the cooling towers. Not too many of them get to use any of the electricity, and some days you have to turn car lights on because of the heavy smoke that hangs over Soweto from the coal-stove fires they use for heat and light.'

I was quiet as he rambled on with facts and figures. It was obvious he was giving me the guided tour first instead of driving straight to our destination. Rows of monotonous boxes – here and there an attempt to cultivate a garden or personalise their homes with a pot of paint. The roads were gravel and strewn with litter. Plastic supermarket bags blew everywhere in the wind, eventually trapping themselves on rusted fence wire.

'Hard to get rid of, those things,' Tom commented, following my gaze. 'But some of the local women have come up with the idea of making them into mats. Some even go overseas. Nothing like exporting your litter, rather than have it blowing around the streets.'

Sure enough, around the next corner was a group of women and children squatting outside a house. Their fingers were deftly knotting yellow *Checkers* bags to the blue and white of *Pick 'n Pay*, and the beige and black of the municipalities; the whole combining to make colourful rugs and mats.

We passed homes belonging to the upper-class Sowetans, which despite their being modern, spacious and neat, were still not up to the standard as Whites of similar business or professional levels.

Eventually we came to an open space at the junction of two mean streets, with a circle of logs spread around a small collection of shacks, forming a stockade. Wooden gates were standing open, and to my surprise Tom drove straight though them.

A few people stood or sat around the cleared space in front of the shacks. They were dressed mostly in Western clothing but a few wore traditional costume, including the large man standing before the open door-

34

way of the largest structure. The interior was gloomy, and nothing could be seen from the outside.

We climbed out of the car and Tom raised a hand in salute. He spoke to the guard outside the 'house', who repeated his greeting of *ukubulisa* and stepped aside. The smell was appalling as we entered and the only light came from a few candles. By their feeble glow I could see a hideous tribal mask on one wall.

'What *is* this place?' I asked softly.

'This is Chele's *kraal*' he said cheerfully. 'He's a witchdoctor.'

'Charming,' I muttered. 'Now you tell me...' I stopped as the mask began to move, the eyes glaring balefully, and I heard Tom's low chuckle as I jumped back.

'You're looking at a *Sangoma*' the American drawled. 'She's an old woman who works for Chele, the main man around here.'

Another voice spoke, seemingly from the wall itself, and the mask melted back towards it. The old woman drew back a heavy dark curtain and a blaze of light flooded the room. I saw the *Sangoma* had a thick cake of mud or ochre on her face surmounted by her long hair, braided with shells and beads. It was no wonder I'd taken her for some hideous mask.

I looked around and shuddered. The room was much bigger than I'd thought, and was filled with the remains of long dead creatures and dried plants. Skulls, legs, hooves, and whole mummified remains, hung from the ceiling. Shelves were fixed precariously on the walls, covered with roots, herbs and burnt leaves. The stench was foul and the atmosphere was no better than a humid dustbin.

I followed Tom's tall figure as he stooped to pass under the curtain, not knowing what to expect, but certainly unprepared for what I found.

Six

My first impression was of a lecturer's room at Cambridge. It was not large, but every available space had been well used. Shelves lined the walls from floor to ceiling, every one laden with books, from paperbacks to leather bindings. Behind them you could barely make out the dark panelling that matched the shelving.

The centre of the room was taken up with a huge partner's desk, such as those favoured by solicitors.

Seated behind it was a black man in his mid-forties, immaculately attired in a cream lightweight suit, a white silk shirt, and a dark tie that bore a college motif. On our side of the desk were two comfortable wing-backs, matching the one he was seated in.

The man rose, and although he was of medium height, his shoulders were wide and gave an impression of power. He moved around the desk and threw his arms about the tall American. Tom returned his embrace warmly, before stepping back and introducing me.

'Phillip Christie O'Brien, meet Chele Mopane, the owner of this fine emporium, which mightn't look much but is like having his own gold mine, or a licence to print money.'

The well-dressed man came forward with a smile and took my hand. He was going bald at the front and wore glasses. I could see his eyes glinting with amusement as he shook my hand in a strange way. He grasped my hand as usual, then wrapped his fingers around the thumb, and returned to the normal grip. I learned later that this was the traditional Zulu handshake and those used overseas are a corruption of this.

'The pleasure is mine, Phillip,' he said. His English was excellent, with a hint of American accent. He returned to take his seat behind the desk.

'Neat set-up, eh, Phil?' Tom lowered his long frame into one of the comfortable wingbacks and I took the other. 'Outside for the peasants, in here for the more sophisticated hypochondriacs.'

'You certainly have a way with words, Tom,' Mopane winced. 'A pity you don't know what they all mean.'

He turned his gaze in my direction. 'I'm a medical doctor, Phillip, not a witch doctor as our giraffe-like friend here would have you believe. My people have been *inyangas* for many generations, and I was sent to the States to train as a modern doctor. That was were I first met Tom.'

He rose and swung out a section of bookcase, revealing a small, but well-stocked, bar. 'Scotch and soda okay?' he asked and we both nodded. After Tom Jackson's version of Margaritas I was grateful for anything.

'I had already served my apprenticeship as an *inyanga*, and when I returned I took over from my father,' I heard the hiss of a soda maker. 'Here I combine the knowledge of both worlds – the ancient and the modern. I am a First World doctor with Third World roots. Many Western medical people are beginning to take notice of the treatments used by the *sangoma* and *inyanga*.'

I asked him what the difference was.

'The *sangomas* are diagnosticians and diviners, mainly women,' he replied, handing us our drinks and resuming his seat. 'They are consulted about why certain calamities have happened. Why the cows are barren; why the fields are not producing crops; or why a young bride is not yet pregnant. They are great psychologists, with a fine understanding of the human mind. Patients often come in large groups, and the *sangoma* can throw the bones, or interpret the hand or stick clapping of the crowd.'

He paused and we all took a sip of our drinks. Chivas Regal. Doctor Mopane couldn't be doing too badly for himself.

'The *inyanga* – or *izinyanga* to give its correct name – is the healing doctor, usually a man, who specialises in natural treatment methods. We use herbs and plants, bark, animal fats, minerals, skins, roots, leaves and animal horn. It is estimated there are about 120,000 traditional healers in South Africa alone.'

He paused to let it sink in.

'My "peasant" patients – as our crude friend here refers to them – expect to come to a place like the next room. They want to taste the traditional atmosphere as they sit opposite the *sangoma* and tell their stories. A pain somewhere: unrequited love, faithless love. Everything in the healing world is dealt with in my *kraal*. Everything in the darker world of revenge and hatred is dealt with by the *abathakathi*, the wizards and witches. They are feared because of their knowledge of poisonous plants, and will kill without compunction. Hair is never left around after a haircut, for the *abathakathi* will use it to drive the person insane. Likewise a person's urine or excreta can be used to cast spells against him.'

I looked up from my drink to see if he was serious or not. There was certainly no smile on his face.

'Come on, Chele,' Tom chuckled. 'You don't really believe that stuff, do you?'

'I've seen things I cannot explain,' he answered simply. 'You must understand, my friends, that since the dawn of time religion has always formed an integral part of African life. They do not have shrines, temples or monuments because the African people have never worshipped inanimate objects, unlike the so-called superior culture of the white man. Religion is for everyday living, with the focus on a supreme and invisible being, known by different names to different tribes. It is *Tixo* to the Xhosa, *Tilo* to the Tsonga, *Modimo* among the Sotho, and *Umvelinqangi* to the Zulu. These are the people who come next door, or sit outside in the *kraal*.'

He sipped slowly and smiled at us both. 'This room is for the other people who come for help; Whites, Chinese, Asian, and sophisticated Blacks. Many use our healing methods, but not all will admit to it. Many Western doctors are two-faced. They ridicule traditional healers, yet many of our beliefs have been validated by science. Green herbs are quack medicine, but grind it into a white powder and they regard it as a revolutionary cure. Now, I understand you have some questions concerning the death of a friend?'

I shook myself back to the present, mesmerised by his words. Tom had obviously been in touch with him, so I spoke briefly of John Barnes – how he was working for *Sable* magazine as a reporter – and the official police verdict of his terrible death. I hinted there was perhaps something sinister behind their refusal to allow me to examine the case file.

'I don't think so,' Tom shrugged. 'It's normal police procedure not to let people have access to official files. If you were a relative, and went through a lawyer... maybe. But not in the circumstances.'

'The major I spoke to said that John had been killed for parts of his body but wouldn't elaborate on it,' I said carefully. 'I looked up the word you muttered last night, Tom. *Muti*. It means 'medicine', and I remembered reading something last year about a small boy being mutilated for medicine. Surely that's not true, is it?'

'Yes Phillip, it is true,' the doctor said slowly. 'I wish it were not. A three year old boy was found on the veld outside Soweto. His penis, testicles and thumbs had been cut off. He had also been cut around the eyes in an attempt to remove them. Surgeons have been performing sex change operations to turn him into a girl.'

'My God,' I breathed. 'Why...?'

'As you said: medicine.' He finished his whisky and collected our glasses to replenish them. I did not refuse. 'I'm afraid the simple minds of my people believe that the human body is the best form of *muti*, especially the sexual organs. That little boy was Black, but Whites are considered much better.'

'There was a case a few years ago where a White kid went into a public toilet during broad daylight, and a Black guy followed him in and cut off his pecker and balls,' Tom said harshly. 'Not long after – or it could have been before, I forget – there was a White woman who crossed a small section of bushland on her way home from a friend's house. She never made it. They found her strung out between two trees. What was left of her.'

He took a sip of his whisky while I gulped mine. Surely they were putting me on...

'That's not the worst part. The grass in front of where they killed her was flattened over a wide area.'

'You mean...?'

'That's right,' he looked into my eyes. 'There was a big audience watching them take her apart. And we're not talking about the serial killer sickos you find in the US and Britain.'

'Who all happen to be White,' I pointed out.

'Ok, so they're *mostly* White, but they're nuts and everyone knows it. These people aren't nuts, they just happen to be fuckin' primitive. But they *listen* to the ones who are nuts, and do what they tell them. That's the worrying bit. It's like the Mau Mau all over again.'

There was silence for a while. I felt sick, and knew it wasn't the Chivas Regal.

'It is not easy for strangers – Black or White – to understand the Black people of this land, Phillip,' Chele

40

Mopane said. 'I use the word "strangers" without reservation, for often my Western education puts me outside their simple world.'

'Simple...' I breathed. 'How simple do you have to be to do something like that to people. They must hate the Whites a lot.'

'On the contrary, it's because they respect them that they do such things. They respect their strength and their cleverness, and think these attributes can be ingested in the form of *muti* and so cure their problems. Much as in the old days the warriors would eat the heart of a lion to take on his ferocity and power.'

'Or the Apache who would torture his prisoner to death to see how long it took him to die,' Tom added drily. 'The longer it took, the greater the man. Therefore the greater the captor.'

Mopane nodded. 'Unfortunately we are all gathered under the same banner. Very few *sangoma*s or *inyangas* are involved in these things. It is the work of the *abathakathi*.'

'In Pretoria recently three Blacks went on trial for the killing of a White man,' Tom nodded. 'They'd cut off his head and genitals for medicine. The one who'd ordered it was a witchdoctor, and he was so cocky they'd buried the body a few metres from his house.'

'Phillip,' Chele frowned. 'Despite everything we've said here, I do not believe that this man was killed for *muti*. Tom, does your journalist's mind recall the reports when the body was found?'

'Sure,' the American nodded. 'It was just before I went back to the States. I did a small by-line on it myself.'

'Can you describe *where* it was found?'

'Just on the side of the motorway. The N12.'

'How *far* from the side?'

'Couple of yards, I guess, but what...?'

'Too close not to be seen by the lights from passing cars, if someone was being killed and butchered in that spot?'

'Well, sure,' Tom frowned. 'But the body was wrapped in a black bin liner, and there was little blood found at the scene...'

'Exactly,' Chele prodded the air with a finger. 'Remember the story you told of the White woman before? She was killed and dismembered *on the spot*. That is very important to the body having any efficacy as *muti*. John Barnes was killed and cut up elsewhere than the place he was found, otherwise the ground would have been covered with his blood. And why else would they put his remains in a sack – if not to transport it from another place?'

We both stared at him. That oafish detective van Zyl could have learned a lot from this man.

'Sounds like he was dumped out of a car,' Tom said in disgust. 'Why didn't the cops catch on to that one?'

'They did not ask,' Chele Mopane said softly. 'Also, although no-one knows in advance about these killings, I hear about them later. The word goes around that a certain healer has good *muti*, and the people flock to him.'

'That's that,' I said wearily. 'There's no way we can trace an unknown car that dumped a body from a motorway back in May.'

'Maybe we don't have to,' Tom sat up straight. 'The body was chopped up to put the cops off the scent. It was made to look like a *muti* killing to cover the fact that Barnes was murdered for another reason.'

'What other reason?' I was interested.

'What story was he covering at the time?' Tom countered. 'Find out and I bet it leads to his killers.'

Seems simple enough,' I said doubtfully. 'Why do I have the feeling it won't be?'

'Because you're a born pessimist, my Limey friend,' Tom grinned and rose to his full height, his head scraping the ceiling. 'Chele, thanks for the drinks and the talk.'

Chele Mopane, medical doctor and *inyanga*, shook hands with both of us in turn. 'I hope I've cleared up a few things for you Phillip, and please don't think too harshly of my people. Think of them as children, as I do. The privilege of education is a large responsibility.'

I turned to go, not sure if I really wanted to hear excuses for such horrors, whether performed through ignorance or otherwise.

'One last thing,' he said. 'The town near where he was killed, Potchefstroom. There was a BWB march through the town in May, around the time your man was killed, and he might have been covering that. If they saw him they would not have liked it. It might be worth looking into but I should be very careful, Phillip. Very careful.'

I made no reply, and we took our leave. As we drove away from Soweto I was silent. For I had seen a frightened look in Chele's eyes, and knew he was not a man who frightened easily.

Seven

Thousands of khaki-clad farmers marched down the main street of Potchefstroom, bringing traffic to a halt.

'The basies (bosses) are angry,' a black messenger on his scooter made the sign of the cross. 'They are angry and they do not play with people. The big war is coming, and God must help us.'

Finally he wrapped his courage around him like a cloak and bravely weaved his way through the flag-waving, placard-carrying crowd. He disappeared amidst roars of laughter and racist jokes.

They came from all over the country; in expensive cars, four-wheel drive vehicles, bakkies and buses, to vent their nationalist anger in the 150 year old Transvaal town.

They sang *Sarie Marais* at the tops of their voices as they marched towards the Olen Stadium, past the Old Powder Magazine and the Fort built by the British in 1880. They wanted the world to know that they would not live under an ANC government.

The crowd was angry because of the murder of farmers, the Basic Conditions of Employment Act for farm labourers, the possibility of the security forces being placed under multi-party control, and the threatened occupation of white schools.

As they made their way between the long lines of traffic they had brought to a standstill, a tall blond farmer with a toy pistol stopped at a truck. He held the pistol to the head of the black driver and shouted, *'Kaffir, ons gaan vir jou doodskiet'*, (Kaffir, we're going to shoot you dead').

The crowd cheered and the farmers' wives screeched with laughter. The Klipdrift brandy and Coke was already flowing.

As they slowly filed into the stadium, home of the Western Transvaal rugby team, the sun beat down and the temperature rose to 32 degrees. 6,000 farmers from the heartland of South African agriculture sat and waited for the rally to begin, so they could voice their demands in unison.

When they did it brought to mind the Hitler rallies of the 30s. They bayed for blood. They booed the government as traitors, and forced the Deputy Agriculture Minister, Tobie Meyer the younger brother of Roelf Meyer the chief government negotiator, to abandon his speech.

'Skiet hom,' they cried. 'Send him home. Get rid of the traitor'. The SA Agricultural Union president, Boet Fourie, had less chance of being heard and resumed his seat as a defeated man.

As the speeches became more fiery, members of the *Blanke Weestandsbeweging* (White Opposition Movement) made loud and repeated calls for war. A handful of AWB supporters in full uniform bore their triple-seven flag.

Amid the smell of *braaivleis* and *boerwors* came the calls for Afrikaner unity, mobilisation, and armed conflict..."

I put the micro-fiche display on hold. The article was from the evening edition of Thursday the 6th May. I was about to go for a coffee when my eye caught the bottom of the column.

...stepped into the crowd where a Black man was taking photographs of the march. During the ensuing fracas the man sustained slight injuries and his camera was damaged.
  Witnesses report the man kept trying to tell the khaki-clad farmers he was a reporter but they would not listen to him..."

That was it. It had to have been John Barnes. Not satisfied with beating him up and breaking his camera they'd found him later, and dished out the ultimate punishment.

I punched out a copy and left the building. I'd insisted on Tom dropping me off when we got back into town, and the article I'd just read confirmed the words of Chele Mopane.

I caught a taxi to the intersection of Market and Nugget streets, from where I had directions to meet Tom in a small Chinese restaurant.

On the corner itself was the Madressa Himayatil Islam mosque, built in 1916 and since enlarged and modernised. I smiled when I read the board outside. The tower, 30 metres high, is equipped with a public address system in order to save the *muezzin* from climbing for the five daily obligatory calls to prayer. It also has a floor that is electrically heated for the comfort of the devout while praying. Religion made easier for the masses.

I found the restaurant easily enough, though I did have a little difficulty in finding Tom at first. He was sitting with his back to me over on the far wall. To be fair, it was the blonde lady sitting opposite him that had put me off.

I didn't expect him to have company, and

certainly nothing like the woman he was with – mid-thirties and beautiful. She'd obviously been briefed of my impending arrival for she smiled and murmured a few words to her companion. Tom looked around and waved.

After the introductions were made he poured me a glass of red wine and I sipped slowly, trying to work out the situation. Her name was Marike Geldenhuys, and surprise, surprise, she too was a journalist.

'Actually I'm a photo-journalist,' she corrected, when Tom said they'd known each other a long time, and were in the same game. Their close friendship was evident from the easy way they rubbished each other's remarks. I wondered if there was something more there.

'So, how did the search through the files go?' Tom enquired, and I knew he was being patronising by the gleam in his eye.

'Very well,' I said smugly, then hesitated.

Tom smiled and nodded at Marike. 'Don't mind her. She knows it's my story if anything breaks. Anyway, she might be able to help.'

I felt myself frowning slightly. I hadn't really thought about Tom's motives before. I'd naively assumed he was helping me from the kindness of his heart. Then I remembered that journalists weren't supposed to have hearts.

'I think Chele could be right,' I said, deciding Tom might as well get the story as anyone. I showed him the article, and exchanged small talk about Johannesburg with the blonde while he read it.

He passed it across the table when he'd finished and she merely glanced at it and gave it back to me.

'Yes, I covered it myself for a British magazine. I also saw the poor man being attacked. Four men jumped out of the march and started jostling him around, calling him filthy names and threatening him in Afrikaans.'

'You speak Afrikaans?' I asked in surprise.

'Of course,' she looked straight at me and I saw her eyes were the greenest I'd ever seen on a blonde. Surely they belonged to a redhead. There again, maybe she *was* a redhead. In which case why would she want to...

'...I *am* Afrikaans,' her voice cut across my irreverent thoughts. 'They dropped his camera on the ground and made a big thing of "accidentally" stepping on it. They're pigs, Mr O'Brien, but growing up on a farm in the Western Transvaal I can understand their feelings. I don't condone the actions of any of these neo-Nazi groups, but a lot of history is behind what they want, and consequently what they do.'

'I think I understand. Your people colonised this land,' I was aware too late of how condescending the words must have sounded.

'Colonised it, forced a living from it, fought for it, and many of them died for it,' she said quietly. 'No, Mr O'Brien, you *don't* understand. How can you? You're an educated Black man who comes from a nation that has always advocated equality, even though some might not practice it. Unlike Tom, whose people are still second class citizens in many parts of *his* country.'

She began fiddling with the condiments and I thought she'd finished. I was about to speak when she began again.

'Unless you were raised in this country you can never understand it, nor our people. And I mean *all* of our people, Coloured and Indian, as well as Black and White. After years of struggle, and yes, I admit they have had some good years too, now there is the threat that their land will be taken from them and split up among the Blacks.'

Again I was about to open my mouth, but some instinct of survival made me look at Tom and he smiled and shook his head slightly. I closed it again.

'You only have to look at their record to know how damaging that would be to the agricultural business in this country. Agronomists from all over the world have come here to try and teach them correct farming methods in the homelands. Our own government, despite what the rest of the world thinks, has spent millions of rand doing the same.'

She looked up from her fiddling and gave a smile of self-deprecation. 'I'm sorry, I'm waffling on again. Tom should have warned you what I'm like when I get on my hobby-horse.'

'Could be you know too much about everyone,' the American said quietly. 'The good as well as the bad, so you feel pretty mixed up about things. Marike speaks fluent Zulu and Xhosa,' he said to me.

'I grew up among the Xhosas on my father's farm, and spent most holidays at my uncle's in Zululand. I love the Zulus, but I have no illusions about them. They're a fierce people.'

Again that hesitation, a child-like quality of uncertainty, yet I knew that wasn't it. 'You can't understand the frustration of a *Boer* who has to tell a worker the same thing every day for a year before he grasps it. Or before he wants to. The Zulu sees himself as a warrior – not a farmer or herdsman – yet he has to do those jobs these days. He's quite happy to sit outside his *rondavel*, smoking *dagga* and talking to his cronies while his wives do all the work. Good God, is that the time. I've got to run.'

We stood as she picked up her handbag. I had a feeling of loss, for I was interested in what she had to say. It was the grass-roots kind of stuff I was here for. Despite that she was a White.

'Good-bye, Mr O'Brien,' she held out a deceptively fragile hand that had strength in it. 'I'll see what I can find out about John Barnes, but a friendly suggestion if I may? I wouldn't advise going to Potchefstroom and poking around. I'll give you a ring, Tom.'

With that she swept out of the restaurant and it felt like summer had left and autumn was closing in. Poetic I know, but that was the way I felt at the time.

Tom must have noticed something in my expression, for he topped my glass up and sat back with a cynical look in my direction.

'She'll break your heart, man. She might be a liberal, White female, with no racial prejudices to speak of – and believe me she *is*, and she *hasn't*. But she's still an Afrikaner born and bred and I shouldn't think a romantic clinch with a Black man figures too high on her social calendar.'

'Tom, I wasn't even thinkin...'

'I know what you "weren't even thinkin", buddy, and I recognised the look in your eyes. Believe me, it's natural. I used to have the same look myself when I first met her. She's a lovely lady, in any colour, and she happens to be a nice one too. We go back a long way, Marike and me. We've covered some hairy situations together, like Beirut and Belfast, and we've got drunk in each other's company many times, but I'll tell you one thing. There was never a time that I didn't know exactly where I stood with her. I hate to be crude, Phil, but Black cock ain't what she hankers after.'

'Well,' I was completely deflated after all that. 'You certainly told me. I'm glad I didn't ask.'

'Hey, I'm sorry, pal,' he grinned. 'What say we eat something? I'm starved. You can keep your soul food, I'm into Chinese.'

'Chinky nosh,' I murmured.

'What?'

'Chinky nosh,' I explained. 'It's what we call it in Liverpool. I had a Chinese friend, very wealthy parents. It always made us smile when he suggested we go for a "chinky".'

Tom smiled and nodded politely, but he hadn't really been listening. His mind was on other things.

'You intend to poke your nose into Potchefstroom, don't you? Despite Chele and Marike warning you to keep the hell away?'

For some reason I was feeling down, which likely prompted my answer. Maybe I'd been planning it since I'd read the article.

'Tomorrow,' I drained my glass. 'I intend to go tomorrow.'

'Correction, friend.' The grin was back again. Not that it ever went far from Tom's face. '*We* are going tomorrow.'

He would brook no argument on the subject, and refused to discuss it. We enjoyed an excellent meal, washed down with another bottle, and talked of other things. Tom explained that he'd had to give up a promising basketball career because of bad knees.

'Besides, I wouldn't have got too far in the majors today. Too goddamn short.'

I laughed at the absurdity of his remark but he assured me it was true. 'These guys today are something else, man. They *start* at seven foot, and there's one player who's nearly 8 freakin' foot high *and* he's a *White* guy to boot. Doesn't that beat all?' He shook his head in disbelief.

He went on to regale me with tales of his days as a player, and some of his adventures as an international journalist. 'Always found it hard to get lost in the crowd,' he grinned. 'But I could always reach the tape-recorder over their heads when I asked a question.'

More than once during the meal I felt glad he'd changed the subject. I wasn't looking forward to the next day, and that night I had nasty dreams of enormous khaki-clad Whites surrounding me, all pointing rifles in my direction. Only when they pulled the trigger, instead of bullets it was basketballs that came hurtling at me. When they got close I saw they weren't basketballs at all, but huge grinning skulls.

More than once I woke up covered in sweat.

Eight

The Voortrekkers were expecting a fresh attack, but when it came it shocked them all. Thundering towards them through the bush came the Ndebele secret weapon. It was a cavalry charge, but unlike any other cavalry charge in history. The hardy Boers stood dangerously still in awe as the warrior-mounted oxen pounded towards them.

The oxen had been specially trained and their horns sharpened to rip the flanks and bellies of the Voortrekkers' horses.

It was November 1837 and near the end of what would be known as the Nine Days Battle; the final showdown between the Voortrekkers and the Ndebele chief, Mzilikazi.

Andries Hendrik Potgieter had mustered a force of 330 men and set out to defeat the troublesome Mzilikazi once and for all. There was a series of bitter clashes in which the Ndebele suffered heavy losses and their villages were in flames.

On the sixth day of the battle, Mzilikazi made his last desperate bid for victory by sending in the oxen cavalry. There was a wild moment when he almost succeeded, but then the Boers began to fight for their lives, and the noise of battle and the smell of blood overwhelmed the terrified oxen. They stampeded back through the bush, goring and trampling their masters.

For three days the Voortrekkers chased the shattered army northwards, for the power of Mzilikazi in the Transvaal was broken. He fled across the Limpopo to the land which would one day be called after a great city out of Africa's past. Zimbabwe.

Mzilikazi re-established his people on the high central ridge and called their new country Matabeleland.

Andries Potgieter followed his victory in the Nine Days Battle by founding a town in 1838, and he called it Potchefstroom. It became the capital of the South African Republic and today is the oldest European town in the Transvaal.

Potchefstroom has the dubious distinction that on the 16th December 1881, the first shot was fired there during the Boer War.

I was pleasantly surprised when we drove through the town, for those early settlers had planned it well, with broad streets aligned along the points of the compass. Traditional Cape Dutch existed peacefully alongside Victorian, with the austere practicality of the post-war years intruding on the charm of the early settlers.

We drove past the University for Christian Higher Education, founded by the Dutch Reformed Church, and I wondered how such strong regard for religion equated with the article I'd read the day before. The thought stayed in my mind as we passed the music conservatory, the library, and the museum. A sign pointed the way to Lakeside, a leisure resort on the Mooi River which boasted swimming, boating, fishing, and chalets.

'Fancy spending the night in a chalet on the river?' I asked. 'Or do you prefer a hotel? Apparently the town has several.'

'Neither,' Tom shook his head. 'I don't think staying the night is a good idea, man. I'd like to head back when we've asked a few questions.'

I looked at him in surprise.

'Speaking of which, what say we hit that place over there and start enquiring?' He pointed to a hotel on the corner of two streets.

'Fine with me,' I nodded.

I expected him to park outside but Tom drove a block away and parked down a side street. He winked as he locked the car and we strolled back. He ignored the main entrance, with its sign proclaiming LADIES BAR: REASONABLE DRESS ONLY, and we went around the corner to the sign that said PUBLIC BAR, with no stipulation on dress.

It was 6pm, and the bar was filled with workers who'd just finished for the day. They were mostly Blacks but there were a few Coloureds sitting at tables against the walls.

The bar staff consisted of a surly looking White, and two Blacks. They were dispensing drinks as if the warning signs were out, and the brewery was going on strike the next day.

'These are the lucky ones,' Tom said from the side of his mouth. 'They've all got jobs, but look what they do with their money. Piss it up against the wall.'

We had no problem pushing up to the bar, as we both towered over the other patrons.

'*Ja?*' the White barman had decided we looked affluent enough to command his personal attention.

'Hi there, bro,' Tom used his exaggerated streets-peak. 'Two beers and a moment of your time, m'man. Back in May, when they had the big march, we mislaid a friend. Maybe you've seen him around?'

'Bit shorter than me, light-skinned Black chap,' I added.

The fat-gutted man behind the bar, who could have walked into a lead part in *Night of the Living Dead* without make-up, gave us a look of contempt. He muttered, 'Two beers, *ja*,' and wandered away.

'Friendly kinda guy,' Tom commented, and turned to face the room. Everyone was watching us, some surreptitiously, some staring openly.

When the drinks came Tom paid for them and began circulating, drink in hand. He stopped here and there, smiling and talking. I went in the other direction but it was clear from the start that no-one there was going to say a word to the two strangers. It was either a blank stare, or 'no English, baas' from the Blacks.

We met back at the bar and Tom shrugged. 'Waste of time, Phil, they ain't talkin. Let's try the Ladies Bar.'

I felt twenty pairs of eyes follow us as we left.

'By now that pot-bellied weasel of a barkeep will be diving around to this side to tell them we're coming,' Tom said conversationally. We walked into the Ladies Bar, so called because they were supposed to be well-appointed lounges where ladies could visit on their own. Previously it just wasn't done.

'Two beers, please,' I used an intimidating posh accent.

One of the lines from Shaw's Pygmalion goes, 'It is impossible for an Englishman to open his mouth, without making some other Englishman despise him.'

He's right. Unless you're Black, then it doesn't matter how you speak, someone will despise you anyway. I've found a more upper class accent than usual, makes people despise you for that, and not so much for your colour. Combined, they get beneath the skin of most bigots.

The barman was a bigger version of the one next door. He was at the far end of the bar talking to a large red-necked individual seated on a stool. When I ordered, the barman's head turned slowly and he examined us both, slowly and insultingly. He obviously found us wanting, for he deliberately went back to his conversation.

When the American's brows began to meet in the middle, I did not need to be clairvoyant to know he was 'about to lose his cool', as he would say. I looked around the room. About a dozen men, all White, all 'reasonably dressed', some more so than others.

Tom strolled along the bar, and only when he got close to the standing barman did anyone realise how big he really was. It wasn't just his height, but since his basketball days he'd put on a lot of weight and he was most impressive close up.

'My friend asked for some drinks,' his deep voice rang out. 'Do you have a problem with that?'

'I'm busy,' the man replied, without taking his eyes off the person across the bar. 'You'll 'ave to wait, man.'

The way he said 'man' made it sound derisory, whereas Tom used it as a term of endearment. Not looking at Tom when he spoke to him was another mistake.

A long arm shot out, and a hand that could hold a basketball grabbed the man's shirt. He was jerked hard against the bar, only his paunch tucking in beneath it stopping him from joining us on this side.

'You've got no manners, friend,' Tom growled. 'Or else you're refusing to serve us. *Are* you refusing to serve us, asshole?'

The man's head began to shake in denial, before his right fist came over the counter in a punch designed to take Tom's head off. The tall man made no move except to straighten his arm and push him back so the blow sailed harmlessly past. Unlike Tom's left, which didn't sail past, and certainly wasn't harmless.

There must have been nearly 300lbs behind that punch, and the barman took it full in the mouth. The fact that Tom still held on to his shirt did nothing to cushion the blow, and only when he released it did he slip to the floor.

I knew nothing until the oft clichéd *steel bands* went around my chest, locking my arms uselessly to my side. From the corner of my eye I could see that a pair of shoulders were in line with mine, so a 'reversed Kirkby kiss' from my schooldays was quite in order. The back of my head flattened a nose flush with the rest of the face, and the howl of anguish almost deafened me.

As the arms encircling mine went limp, I spun and sunk a low right into his stomach. As he went down another man came in from the side and I ducked and threw a jab in his face, following it with a right cross that sent him reeling backwards.

I glanced across at Tom and he appeared to be doing fine. As he let the barman go, the man on the stool grabbed hold of his arm. Tom clamped a massive hand over the other man's and kicked the stool from under him, swinging him head first into the bar as he did. He now held his next two attackers behind their necks and was having fun banging their heads together.

The other customers had been enjoying it, but now realised the uppity *kaffirs* were winning. They would be joining in soon.

'Time to go,' I yelled at Tom. 'I don't think they're ready to be interviewed yet.'

Tom laughed and dropped his bundles on the floor. I made for the door, in front of which a bearded man stood holding a large wooden club. His lips drew back in a grin or a snarl as he raised the weapon.

I plowed in with a series of lefts and rights to the head, and he staggered back under the weight. I kept on going as he fell through the door into the street, and kicked him once as I leapt over him. I heard Tom behind me, still laughing, and the sickening sound of bone crunching as he hit someone coming out of the door.

I heard the squeal of brakes and a woman's voice yelling loudly to get in. I needed no urging, for they were spilling out behind us, and I jumped into the front seat and pushed the back door open.

Tom reached for the smallest of his attackers and used him as a scythe to clear a semi-circle in front of him. Once he had some space he hurled the man into the rest and dived into the car.

We spun away in a cloud of burning rubber.

'Just like the movies, huh?' Tom laughed from the back seat, and the driver began to swear at him in several languages.

Nine

'Who taught you to drive, Stevie Wonder?'

Marike Geldenhuys, photo-journalist and rally driver, ignored me. 'I told you not to come here on your own. Tom, you of all people should have known better.'

'You *suggested* it, if you remember. You didn't actually *tell* anyone,' I said snootily, not used to being ticked off like a naughty schoolboy. Even if it was deserved.

'Well, if you can't accept a suggestion, perhaps you *should* be told in future.' She managed to sound just as snooty.

'There won't be a next t...' I began.

'Hey, we didn't go there looking for trouble, girl,' Tom defended us both. 'We were being cool, asking a few questions and then the dudes jumped us.'

'It was decidedly *un*-cool, man,' the corners of her mouth quirked slightly. 'You happened to pick the main hangout of the BWB. You were lucky to get out of there in one piece.'

'Luck had nothing to do with it,' Tom chuckled from the back seat. 'We just gave a whole new meaning to the term "nigger bashing", 'cos *we* did the bashing. My man here is one helluva handy guy with his mitts when he gets upset.'

'University champ,' I said modestly. 'You weren't

59

too bad yourself.'

'Comes from years of playing a non-contact sport,' he laughed.

'Actually I abhor violence of any kind,' I said in an affected voice, and this cracked him up some more.

We drove out of Potschefstroom on the Lakeside road, then suddenly turned onto a gravel drive to the left. It was well-maintained, and after a while the wire fences on either side turned into lines of mature poplars.

'I guess the lady will let us into her confidence when she feels the time is right,' Tom said in a loud voice. 'But I'd like to remind her that I left a car back there.'

'It will be quite safe,' Marike told him. 'Knowing you, it will be parked down a side street miles away from the hotel, and none of your sparring partners will have seen you in it. Don't worry, we'll pick it up on the way back.'

'Way back from where?' I asked.

'A man I know. He's an old friend of my father. A farmer. Actually he's my godfather. He also happens to be one of the leaders of the *Volksfront*.'

'Meaning the white Afrikaner type people, of course?' Tom muttered.

'That's right,' Marike agreed. 'But Jannie Grobbelaar is both an intelligent and reasonable man. He's not one of the militant right-wing who are becoming extremely violent. There have been bomb explosions at Bronkhorstspruit, Patensie and Queenstown; a quantity of R1 rifles stolen from the SADF at Kimberley; and plots to sabotage the Koeberg nuclear power station. All believed to be the work of radical Whites. But Jannie will tell you this himself.'

The drive suddenly terminated in front of an open lawn and we followed the turning circle around to a beautiful Cape Dutch farmhouse.

A man was waiting on the verandah, known in South Africa as the *stoep*, and he hugged Marike warmly. I did not know what Tom's expectations were of this member of the *Volksfront* hierarchy, but if they were anything like mine he couldn't have been more wrong.

He shook our hands and invited us to be seated at a cloth-covered table. The sun was behind the house yet it was still pleasantly warm. He offered us the choice of tea or something stronger – we looked at each other and smiled.

While Jannie Grobbelaar mixed whisky and sodas, Marike gabbled away in Afrikaans, and he began to laugh delightedly and nod his head. The way he looked at us appraisingly, I assumed she'd been telling him about our visit to the local hostelry.

'Sounds like you stirred our little town up somewhat, gentlemen,' he chuckled. He was a tall, spare man, and looked more like an academic than a farmer. Which was exactly what he was. He'd been a professor of English literature at Stellenbosch University, before retiring and taking over the family farm after his brother died.

When I queried his choice of discipline he laughed. 'My mother was English,' he said, and his accent showed hardly a trace of Afrikaans. We talked of university life for a while, comparing the gentle world of academia to the political arena outside.

'Marike tells me you had no luck with your enquiries in town,' he said finally, and there was a twinkle in his eyes. 'I'm afraid you came across our worst elements. They have only one thing in mind – war against the Blacks. It seems they met their match in their first skirmish with you two.'

'We caught them unawares,' I put in quickly, before Tom could elaborate.

He poured more drinks and sat back sucking on his pipe. 'So far the police have identified 123 far-right groupings, of which 11 are regarded as significant. These include the AWB, BWB, Boerstaat Party, Right Unity Front, the World Apartheid Movement, etc. Many belong to more than one group, some belong to several, but the danger lies not so much in the organised ones but in fanatical individuals who form "terrorist cells", to challenge what they perceive as a threat to their lifestyle and culture from black people.'

We chewed that one over for a while, and I admitted to being somewhat confused. Before I'd left UK it all seemed very simple. Hordes of khaki-clad Storm-troopers running around giving Nazi salutes and trying to enslave black people.

'No, you're right, Mr O'Brien,' he shook his head sadly. 'It is not that simple. I am not a member of the AWB, who are a lot of fat uncles running around doing silly things like the raid on the World Trade Centre, nor the BWB who would declare war tomorrow. Five of them have been arrested for the arms raid on the SADF depot at Pietersburg. I don't agree with them, but I do believe in the preservation of our Afrikaner heritage, just as the English would preserve their roots in this country.'

He was interrupted by a short grey-haired woman who came bustling out. Tom and I stood and were introduced to his wife. If she was surprised at two black men sitting drinking with her husband and god-daughter she did not show it. She insisted that we eat with them and would call us when it was ready.

'It's what she lives for,' Marike said with a smile when she'd gone back in the house. 'Cooking for people. When there's a wedding in the workers' *kraal* she'll spend all week making the cake and preparing fancy dishes.'

Jannie sat smoking for a while, and we waited politely for him to continue. That he had been a lecturer was evident in his manner of presentation, and I found I was interested in what he had to say.

'Just outside Pietersburg, in the Northern Transvaal,' he said. 'There is a road sign that says *Nirvana*, and it points to the heart of the Waterberg. As far as the white people up there are concerned it means the whole of the Northern Transvaal, for it is their ideal state; the Waterberg in the west, the northern Lowveld in the east, and Pietersburg, the Ysterberg and the Soutspansberg in the middle. It is the land that belongs to the Volk, and the only government they will accept is of the Volk, by the Volk, for the Volk. Naturally it is the centre for the *Volksfront*, and there is talk of secession and of the establishment of a transitional Parliament.'

'You mean a homeland, yet not a homeland like Transkei and the rest?' Tom asked suddenly. 'More like kwaZulu, perhaps?'

'Right, Mr Jackson,' the grey head nodded. 'More like kwaZulu. Buthelezi wouldn't accept a homeland those many years ago when the rest did. He wanted the whole of Natal, to run in conjunction with Whites. The government laughed at him, but the white Natalians didn't laugh. Most of them would have accepted such a move, for it would have prevented what's happening now. He would have left the Whites to head the administration and keep the *status quo*.'

Again I was surprised at how open-minded this man was. This white, Afrikaner, *Volksfront* leader. As though reading my thoughts he met my gaze and smiled.

'You didn't come here to listen to an old man drivel on about the future of his people, in a land that you probably think is more yours than his,' he said – there was no cynicism there, more genuine enquiry.

Marike started to speak, probably in my defence for I had the impression that he was not addressing himself to Tom alone, and I held a hand up in restraint.

'You have me wrong, Professor,' I said, admittedly snivelling by using his defunct title. 'I consider myself one hundred percent English, because that is where I was born, where my father was born, and where several generations before him were born. My name is Irish, presumably because some distant ancestor liked the man he worked for and adopted his name. That we

63

were originally from Africa is obvious, though what part exactly is anyone's guess. So... No, I do not consider this country mine, in any way.'

'Well said,' the twinkle was back in his eye. 'But having read your book on slavery I would have imagined you to have far stronger leanings towards your roots.'

'Understandably,' I admitted, pleased that he'd even heard of the book. 'But it was written two years ago, and I'm beginning to rethink a few of the attitudes I've been carrying around.'

Tom was grinning like a Cheshire cat, and Marike was giving me an odd look. I suddenly felt uncomfortable.

'*He that never changed any of his opinions never corrected any of his mistakes,*' Jannie Grobbelaar quoted. 'And this is certainly the place to correct mistakes. I wish my own people could learn theirs. They cannot accept that this land is *not* theirs exclusively, and they must now make room for the black people to share. Apartheid has been legally dead here for many years, but not in the minds of some Whites.'

'It's still alive and well in my country,' Tom muttered. 'And as for Australia, there are still park benches with *Whites Only* written on them...'

A gong sounded from somewhere in the house and our host rose to his feet immediately. 'The *mevrou* is not one to welcome latecomers to her table,' he said with exaggerated timidity, and we followed him inside.

§

The meal was excellent, if different to anything I'd had before. Green mealie soup was followed by a roast of klipspringer, with vegetables done in the Afrikaner style; sweet potatoes, carrots cooked with brown sugar, pumpkin baked and sprinkled with cheese, gem squash, more green mealies.

'Never thought of eating corn before it got yellow,' Tom observed. 'But these are great.'

64

'They're the staple diet of the Zulus,' Marike said.

'That's the trouble,' Jannie frowned. 'Because it has so many uses they grow hardly anything else, but the soil never gets rotated or fertilized. Between that and their damn goats the erosion of native land is a major problem, and they'd do the same to the rest if they got hold of it.'

'Goats?' I repeated stupidly.

'The plague of mankind from Biblical times,' the retired lecturer growled. 'Why do you think the Far East is desert? Goats. They'll eat anything, denude the land and nothing will grow after them. No wonder the ancients depicted the Devil as a goat.'

'It's his favourite moan,' his wife chuckled. Her English was heavy with accent. 'Don't get him started, for pity's sake.'

She bustled around the table piling more food on our plates, with the command, 'Eat up. Big men like you need nourishment'. Marike caught the look of dismay on my face and laughed softly as her godmother went off to the kitchen muttering about dessert.

'I hope you both have a sweet tooth,' she smiled. 'I have a feeling *koeksisters* is on the menu.'

It was over coffee that the old man brought up the purpose of our visit, 'Your friend, the black reporter,' he said slowly. 'He was attacked by four of the men from the march. You know this, so I won't dwell on it. Except to say that no further harm was done to him after the march. At least, not by our people.'

'I don't wish to be argumentative, sir,' I said. 'But how can you be sure of that?'

'Easily,' he shrugged. 'Because I drove him out of Potchefstroom myself when the march was over. As we left the Olen Stadium I saw him at the gate and apologised to him for the behaviour of the few who got carried away. I promised him safe escort back to Johannesburg and he accepted. He was alright when I dropped him off outside his hotel, and will swear this on oath if I have to.'

We sipped our coffees slowly, brandies suddenly appearing on the table before us. I looked up into Marike's startlingly green eyes and she smiled challengingly.

'I don't think that will be necessary, Professor,' I said. 'But I hope you realise you've knocked me off my stride. When I read about John being jumped on in the crowd, I thought it all fitted together neatly. Handed to me on a plate, you might say.'

'Only now you're confused,' he smiled. 'Because you believe me.'

I raised my brandy glass. 'Of course, sir. But where does one go from here?'

'You don't, feller,' Tom said. 'Looks like the trail's petered out, as the Duke would say. We can ask around his hotel, but apart from that it doesn't look hopeful.'

'Perhaps I can help you there,' our host said suddenly. 'I had a long talk with the young man on the way into Jo'burg, and one of the subjects we discussed was an article he had published in the financial page of the Daily Times.'

'I didn't know John Barnes wrote financial news,' I frowned.

'No, he didn't,' Grobbelaar agreed. 'It was more political really. It dealt with the massive amounts of money, from all over the world, that have gone into the ANC coffers in the form of donations. Your friend's article was asking what happened to that money.'

'Norway has been asking the same question,' Marike put in. 'A few years ago they sent R2 million to the ANC to buy tractors, the first part of a R10 million payment, but they're not happy because no tractors have appeared. Sweden was promised future preferential treatment by Mandela in reward for their "continued financial support", which amounts to over R314 million over the past 20 years.'

'Which is a joke, anyway,' Tom added. 'Neither country has the money to give generous donations to anyone, so they borrow it from the World Bank. And who funds the World Bank? The US, UK, and the more affluent EEC countries, who are already handing out great handfuls to the ANC.'

'How long ago was that article, Professor?' I asked.

'About two weeks ago, I'd say.'

'Long enough for someone to read it, digest it, get mad, and take retaliatory action,' I said in one breath.

'Right, time to get you two back to Jo'burg,' Marike said, looking at her watch. 'First we have to sneak into town and collect your car. Tomorrow you can look up the article and see if it's worth pursuing that line.'

We took our leave, declining Mrs Grobbelaar's invitation to stay the night, and headed back into Potschefstroom.

Despite my own anxieties the car was unknown, unwatched, and therefore, untouched. We thanked Marike and bid her goodnight, with an agreement to meet the following day. She was spending the night with her godparents.

'So, Phil, what did you think of old man Grobbelaar?' Tom asked as we left the town.

'Liberal academic,' I replied. 'Forced into farming, but not really his thing. Also forced to take sides, again not to his liking. I'm sure he wouldn't harm anyone himself, but if there was no other way, he'd give the right order. But he'd have to believe in it.'

'Hmm, quite the trick-cyclist, ain't you, boy?' Tom chuckled. 'Yes, I'm sure you're right, so what makes you think he didn't decide that Mr Barnes wasn't becoming a bit too much of a media nuisance, as far as his people were concerned?'

'The question doesn't even arise at the moment,' I shrugged. 'John wasn't the only reporter at that march, and there's a pretty open press here now, so what did they have to gain by killing him? The story was in print by that evening's edition, so why not hit the Times reporter who wrote it?'

'Sure,' he suddenly agreed. 'I guess you're right. Listen, I'm away early in the morning. I'll be gone for a few days, but stay on as long as you like.'

'Thanks,' I smiled. 'I appreciate the offer. I can't make any plans until I know more about John's accusations against the ANC, though once more, the damage has already been done, and not by him alone.'

'True, but if they *are* the ones behind it, I don't think you'll get very far. These guys close ranks pretty tight, you know.'

'The main thing I'd like to get my hands on,' I said tightly. 'Is the pathologist's report on John Barnes.'

'Leave it with me,' Tom winked. 'I've got a few contacts, but I don't think you're going to learn anything from the PM, buddy. It was probably a robbery done up to look like a *muti* killing.'

He'd changed his tack again, and there was something in the dismissive way he spoke that made me glance sharply at him.

Not for the first time I felt myself questioning Tom Jackson's motives in all this.

Ten

'What was it like?' she asked curiously.

I looked up from buttering a piece of bread roll. 'What was what like?'

'Growing up as a black child in Liverpool.'

I shrugged and popped the bread in my mouth. I chewed slowly, trying to work out what she was getting at. I finally realised she wasn't getting at anything. She simply wanted to know.

'The same as growing up as an Irishman, a Welshman, or even an Indian,' I smiled. 'Probably the Irishman and the Welshman would have had a harder time of it. The Irishman, because although most Liverpudlians can trace their ancestry back across the Irish Sea, they still ridicule anyone with a strong Irish accent. The Welshman, because – despite the Welsh border being only eighteen miles from Liverpool – they are a mystery to Scousers who consider they have no sense of humour and are as mean as hell. No, being Black wasn't a problem. Coming from an affluent home, now *that* was a problem.'

Marike stared at me. 'No-one bothered about the colour of your skin but were against you because you came from a rich home?'

I nodded. 'I went to a private prep, which meant wearing a uniform; with a cap and a collar and a tie.

Between my home and school was a housing estate, and on the other side of my school was the state one. Kids would get on the bus from the housing estate. Kids wearing older brother's and sister's hand-me-downs, shoes too big or too small. Imagine what they thought of a bunch of posh kids with fancy uniforms.'

The waiter arrived with our meals. I'd settled for a good old T-bone and salad, and Marike had a fish called yellowtail on a bed of rice.

Tom had left early the following morning and I'd caught a taxi to the newspaper offices. John Barnes' article had been accusative and detailed, but was no great exposé for anyone who wanted to check what he'd written. They were hard facts that did nothing for the ANC's image of caring for its people, many of whom went hungry in various parts of the country.

This while the top echelon lived in fine houses, drove expensive cars, and lived in luxury. True, old Nelson might deserve a few breaks after being incarcerated for twenty-seven years, but surely the magnificent wedding he gave his daughter, including a banquet for 850 people in Johannesburg's five-star Carleton Hotel, could have gone a long way to feed the multitude.

With such thoughts in mind I tucked into my huge T-bone.

'So you spent your early school years being harassed by white children on the bus?' The reporter in her wouldn't let go.

'Yes and No,' I said evasively. 'Yes I was harassed, but so were all of us who went to the "posh school". But not just by white kids. The black kids felt just the same and gave us a hard time. Somehow it was worse for them to see a black face peering out of a public school uniform. Later, when I was twelve, I went to a public school where I was a boarder. There were some boys who made loud comments about "nig-nogs" and the rest, but it didn't last long. The English are basically quite nice, you know. They want to be seen to be fair in all things.'

She smiled, wryly. 'You must have had some hard times.'

'Not after the first few fights,' I grinned. 'After being bred through generations used to decent food and hard work I wasn't exactly the smallest around. Also my dad had boxed for his college and he pushed me into the boxing squad and later into achieving my varsity blue. He probably became a doctor to make up for the damage he'd caused boxing.'

'Interesting,' she laughed. 'Very interesting, but I can't see how you developed the attitudes that come over in your books. They were nearly banned out here, you know. Ten years before and they wouldn't have stood a chance of getting in the bookshops.'

'As I said last night, I'm changing some of those attitudes. I know it's a lousy excuse, but I was talked into writing that way by Neville, my editor. He also published them, and told me that was what sold books. I know one thing though, this next book will be different. If Neville wants to call me a coconut he's welcome.'

'Coconut?'

'Brown on the outside – white on the inside,' I explained, and she smiled. 'There are far too many issues here to simply say apartheid was terrible and all Whites must be punished. Already I know it's not that simple. Like the death of John Barnes.'

We'd discussed the article in the Daily Times, and Marike agreed it was no great reason for murder.

'It was made to look like a *muti* killing,' she mused. 'That was discounted by Chele, and I agree with him. I wrote an article on witchdoctors once, and it all fits. Similarly with the *broederbond*. I have to go along with Jannie on that.'

'Which leaves the ANC,' I said.

'Not really.' As she shook her head, the heavy blonde hair moved as though in a gentle breeze. 'As we've discussed, I don't think they'd have any cause for retaliation about what many other media people have

71

already said. At the moment the political leaders are trying to keep some control over the armed wing, *uMkhonto we Sizwe*, otherwise known as the MK. It's not easy with all the allegations of ANC prison camps coming out. They wouldn't want this kind of publicity if something went wrong. Besides, I believe Mandela honestly wants to do the right thing for this country.'

'Which leaves us nowhere, in that case,' I murmured, forking the last piece of steak into my mouth. 'Tom said he'd try and get the post mortem report, but he'll be away for a few days.'

'Why didn't you say?' Marike frowned. 'I might be able to get a copy. But why do you want it?'

'I don't really know,' I admitted. 'It was just the look on the detective's face when I mentioned it. Maybe there's nothing in it.'

'Well, we'll have to see, Phillip, won't we?' she smiled and I was lost in those green eyes again.

§

Over the next few days we got to know each other pretty well. I know that's a sweeping statement, but some people are acquainted most of their lives and can't claim to really know the other person. Sadly most of them are married. At first, even though unconsciously, both of us saw the other through the narrow-mindedness of generations of the same colour.

We grew up with the intolerant attitudes of our peers, and mouthing platitudes of denial at dinner-tables did nothing to remove the taint in our hearts.

Marike had more excuse for bigotry than me, yet she had little, in the sense that she knew and understood Blacks. *Her* Blacks, that is, the Blacks of Africa. She loved them, despite knowing their limitations, and their cruelties. She loved them as you would love a lion cub that you'd taken from the wild. Cute, cuddly, capable of reciprocating affection and warmth, but you knew that one day it would be big enough, and fierce enough, to have to return to where it came from; to its fellow creatures of the wild.

Except, as she explained to me, the Blacks of Africa were no longer undomesticated beasts of the bush, for they had been shown the white man's civilisation and comforts, and now had aspirations that were on a much higher plane than the sociologists' mere existence triangle of food, clothing and shelter.

'They've been promised things no-one can provide,' she said in her car one day. 'They see Mandela and the ANC hierarchy living in big houses, driving fancy cars, dressed in designer clothes, and they think they will all have the same after the elections. Many other Blacks in this country have those things too, but they've worked for them, and that's what the uneducated ones cannot see.'

She paused and changed down a gear, then moved left to overtake, or perhaps it should be undertake, though a bad choice of word. The Western Transvaal was a region of vast plains covered with maize fields. The boughs of thorn trees hung heavy with the nests of weaver birds, and isolated farmhouses appeared off the dusty roads.

The hazy little towns and hamlets were dominated by tall, well-filled maize silos, and branch railways carried trains loaded with corn, groundnuts, sunflower seeds, salt, cattle, and dairy produce. It was summer, and the Western Transvaal was a green sea of maize, the endless fields comparable to the great wheatlands of America and Canada.

'The soil here is deep and fertile,' Marike continued. 'Great herds of game roamed here once, hunted by San Bushmen. The Tswana farmed the land then, and they had a civilisation of their own. Complex cities of huts surrounded by low stone walls. Two French missionaries arrived here in 1832 and opened a mission in the Mosega Valley, the first European building in the Transvaal. But within a few months Mzilikazi and his Ndebele came along, the missionaries fled and the

Tswana were driven away. It was turmoil for five years, until the Voortrekkers chased the Ndebele north.'

'I've read about that,' I said. 'Mzilikazi founded the Matebele in Rhodesia.'

'That's right. The Boers took over from the Tswanas and the region became one huge farm, until they found diamonds in the Vaal River, but that's another story. I make no excuses for my people. Their ignorance was contributed to by their interpretation of the Bible, much of which they took literally. The Bible said that the Caananites were inferior, and because they were dark-skinned, the early Dutch treated the Africans as such.'

The same ignorance, I knew, as that possessed by the Liverpool traders when they dealt in black ivory.

'Yes there were cruelties, but only as punishments for what they saw as laziness or obstinacy. The Boers thrashed their workers, but they also thrashed their own children for the same reasons. And there were no black slaves here.'

I opened my mouth to protest, but she shook her head.

'No, Malay slaves were brought in to the Cape from the Spice Isles, and some Hottentots were captured and used to work the land. They interbred, which is where the Cape Coloured comes from, but no Blacks were made into slaves. There *were* no Blacks down south in the early days of settlement here. Most drifted down later to work for the Whites, as many of the Blacks in the north came in to work the mines. The Zulus hated the mines and most refused to go underground, so the work was given to the immigrants.'

Not black and white, I thought once more. Nothing was black and white here. Africa was becoming greyer by the day.

We drove on for a while, nursing our own thoughts. Not for the first time I wondered what my life would have been like if I'd been born to poor black parents in Africa, instead of rich black parents in England.

I was tending to feel guilty of my prejudices towards the white people of my country of birth, aware that I had not been fair. Like the children of the aristocracy who 'dropped out' and lived like hippies because of their imagined sin of being born rich.

But of course they could afford to be, for one day they would inherit the wealth and titles they professed to despise. Not many refused, and I for one had inherited an education and sophistication that no amount of self-imposed poverty could negate.

Nor would I wish to.

Immersed in my thoughts, I slowly became aware that the singing was not the car radio, but Marike singing the words of a tune playing on it.

O bring my terug na die ou Transvaal
Daar waar my Sarie woon,
Daar onder in die mielies by die groen doringboom,
Daar woon my Sarie Marais.

She had a good voice, and somehow its high clarity gave a different sound to the guttural Afrikaans.

'That tune,' I said. 'It sounds familiar.'

She smiled, and sang it again in English.

O take me back to the old Transvaal,
That's where my Sarie dwells,
Down there in the maize lands by the green thorn tree,
That's where my Sarie dwells.

'It's beautiful,' I said, and I meant it. 'But the last time I heard it the words were different.'

She gave me a puzzled look.

'I had a friend in varsity,' I laughed at the memory. 'He was absolutely mad. Came from a succession of generals who could trace their lineage back to the time of Ethelred, and he had no choice but to follow in their footsteps when he left Cambridge.'

'I had a cousin who did the same because his

father and grandfather were career soldiers,' she murmured. 'He was killed on the border. Fanie should
never have gone into the Army. He had the soul of a
poet.'

'What a lovely expression,' I said. *The soul of a
poet...* Anyway, his people had always been cavalry, so
of course Charlie went and joined the Royal Marines,
just to be bloody awkward. I went to his pass-out, at a
place called Lympstone in Devon, and they played that
tune. Apparently it was the regimental march of the
Royal Marines Commando units. The last time I heard
it was in the mess that night, when Charlie and his
cronies sang the unofficial version.'

'Why didn't you join up with him?' she asked. 'Or
did you consider you didn't need to prove anything?'

'I'd like to say "yes" to that,' I admitted. 'But the
fact is they wouldn't take me. Not as an officer, anyway. Like the cavalry, and a few other "prestige" regi-
ments, there were no black officers. The funny thing is,
years later when I was having a drink with Charlie, he
brought up the subject. He told me that among the
men there was more chance of a black officer with a
posh accent being accepted than a white officer who
talked the same as themselves. They once experiment-
ed with short term commissions of working class officers with good university degrees, but the men found it
hard to relate. Reverse British snobbery, they call it.
Butlers have always been the same.'

She smiled in sympathy; with me, not the double
standards of the British.

'It is a mixed up world,' she said, and it was then I
began to feel emotions that hadn't surfaced in a long
time.

The scenery had changed now, for we'd come
around in a circle and had reached the high range of
the Magaliesberg, only an hour from Johannesburg.

We had lunch in the village of Magaliesberg, which
lies in a fertile, sub-tropical valley below the southern
slopes of the range. The mountain, village, and the

river flowing through the valley are all named after Magali, or Mohale, a chief of the Po people in the 19th century. Fruit and tobacco farms were in abundance as we drove past.

Altogether it was one of the most peaceful places I'd ever been to, and I hoped it would remain that way for all time.

We ate in the garden of a small hotel, beneath the towering heights of the berg. The food was good, fresh Magliesberg Trout, but the wine was excellent.

'Wait until you get to the Cape,' Marike said. 'You'll find wines that are comparable to anything that comes out of Europe. I went to university at Stellenbosch, right in the middle of wine-growing country and you wouldn't believe how cheaply we bought good wine for.'

'Lucky you, we had to drink a fiendish brew called "scrumpy", because it was cheap. But what makes you think I'm going to the Cape?' I poured more wine into our glasses. 'It looks like the Barnes business is going to keep me around here for a while.'

'You can't leave without visiting the Cape,' she protested.

'According to Drake, *the fairest cape we saw in the whole circumference of the earth*,' I quoted. 'I'll try, but I'm not here indefinitely, and I've research to do yet.'

'You've not done badly so far,' she pointed out. 'Soweto and Potschefstroom, Chele and old Jannie, not to mention droppings from the informed lips of know-it-all Jackson and yours truly.'

'True,' I laughed. 'I promise I'll try to get down to the Cape of Good Hope, on one condition.'

'Which is?'

'That you'll be my guide,' I said hopefully.

Eleven

As it turned out, I was on my way to Cape Town within days.

Early the following morning I received a call from the police. They were releasing John Barnes's luggage to my care, following a call from his editor, Neville Ndongo. I took a taxi and collected one large suitcase and a Canon portable word processor, and returned to the flat.

A search of his suitcase revealed nothing out of the ordinary, and I would have been surprised if it had. I felt sure the police would have gone through it painstakingly. There was a collection of good clothing, even a white Armani suit and Cardin shirts. John Barnes had been a sartorial dresser. A pair of sports shoes, training kit, toilet bag, underwear. All the usual stuff of a man on the move, and nothing out of the ordinary. The underpants were all black, and too brief for my taste, but that was a personal matter. His wallet was also uninteresting.

Everything had been thrown in the suitcase in an untidy heap, and I assumed that was the work of the police – if the hotel porter had packed it he would have taken more care. What disappointed, and puzzled me, at the same time was the absence of any papers, notebooks and the like.

At university I'd invested in a secondhand Amstrad, which proved to be the best couple of hundred quid I ever spent. If nothing else it gave me an interest in WPs, and so I turned to the Canon with its built-in printer. although somewhat out odf date, it certainly appeared more robust than the later state-of-the-art laptops. I began by examining it, and at first couldn't find the power source. When I did I had my first stroke of luck so far.

The Canon Starwriter comes folded up like a thick briefcase, with a handle that lifts out for carrying. Folding the handle and laying it on that side, I pulled down the top and exposed a compact keyboard and a small screen. I lifted up the top cover to reveal the Bubble Jet printer, then looked at the back to find where the power cord was hiding. By pinching two tabs the back cover dropped into my hand, with the power cord compartment beneath.

As I pulled out the cord my eye caught something shiny on the bottom of the compartment. It was a key, and as I tried to pick it up my finger and thumb slid over it. It was heavily sellotaped and I used a kitchen knife to prise it free. It had the initials HFC and a number stamped on, but it was only after a lengthy search of the telephone books that my overtaxed brain cell came into play.

I remembered the sports gear in the suitcase.

The yellow pages spelled out the initials. The Hillbrow Fitness Club, and it was within walking distance. I was beginning to get somewhere.

The mound of muscles on the desk had other ideas.

'Who?' The word was spat from a face that was positively Neanderthal and which only a mother could show affection for.

'John Barnes,' I repeated patiently. 'He was a member here. I've come to collect some things he left in his locker.'

'What things?'

'I don't know what things,' I found myself talking slowly, like enunciating to a deaf person, or the way an Englishman talks to foreigners. 'But if you show me where the locker room is, we can both find out together.'

'Can't do that,' he growled. I realised I should have simply passed myself off as Barnes in the beginning, but I wasn't used to that sort of thing. Then.

'Why not?' I asked and he must have caught the annoyance in my voice. He became even ruder, if that was possible.

'Because I can't leave the fuckin' desk, that's why. And you don't go down there on your own if you're not a member.'

'I take it by your manner you're not exactly grovelling for customers,' I said coldly.

'Not your kind,' he sneered. 'It's for Transvaalers, and your English accent don't get you in 'ere, man.'

'Perhaps this will get me five minutes,' I gave in and laid two R50 notes on the desk. 'Just as far as the locker room.'

'That's different, man. Why didn't you speak like that in the first place?' the notes disappeared into a tracksuit pocket, and he rifled through a tattered card index box on the counter. 'Barnes, you say? Here we are, Barnes, John. What number, fifty-four?'

He led the way along a corridor and into the men's changing room. A line of metal lockers ran along each wall and the middle was taken up with a double line of benches.

He pointed down the right wall and I wandered over to it. The key fitted, the door opened, and I was the proud possessor of a heavy briefcase. Or so I thought.

'Hey, you can't take that,' an indignant voice came from behind me. 'You said it was sports gear, not a briefcase.'

'I didn't say *what* it was,' I pointed out. 'But there might well be sports kit in it.'

'Open it, then,' he ordered, moving closer.

'Rubbish,' I said, becoming really mad now. 'This is my friend's case and I'm picking it up. Whatever's in it is no business of yours.'

'Well, I'm making it my business...' and he threw a left – into the steel door that I swung out. His bunched fist smashed into it and I could hear bones break. It must have been quite painful, judging by the yell of agony he let out.

I hit him with a straight right of my own, then dropped the briefcase and circled a left hook to the side of his jaw, a punch I'm still quite proud of, and he went down in a heap at my feet. No matter how much muscle they're packing elsewhere, the jaw stays the same. I retrieved my R100 from his pocket. After all, he *had* reneged on the deal. Or tried to.

§

I'd just finished a general perusal of Barnes' papers when Marike proved as good as her word, and appeared at the flat with a copy of the post mortem report. She'd also brought the makings for lunch, and I opened a bottle of wine. While she prepared a tuna salad I sipped a fruity Pinotage and read the report.

I found it on the last page, under the heading of CONCLUSIONS, and read it with a feeling of distaste. Following a detailed examination, the anus of the deceased was found to have an enlarged orifice. There were no fresh ruptures of the fine rectal capillaries, meaning that the enlargement had been caused over a period of many years – indicating regular sexual activity in that area.

John Barnes had been a practising homosexual. No wonder Detective Warrant Officer van Zyl had sneered as he walked out of the office. He thought I was one of the dead man's boyfriends.

I repeated this to Marike as we sat over lunch, and she laughed. 'In that case I feel safe enough to guide you to the Cape.'

81

'Good,' I beamed. 'Because we're going tomorrow.'

She took the news in her stride. 'Rather sudden, isn't it?'

I told her about the briefcase. 'Last month he was in Cape Town, which I understand is the gay centre of Southern Africa.'

'It's not San Francisco, if that's what you mean, but it does have a liberated air about it, compared to Jo'burg, Pretoria or Durban. Which is why a lot of people of alternative preferences tend to gravitate down there.'

'Eloquently put,' I said. 'A simple yes would have sufficed. Aren't you a bit worried that I might be one of them?'

'Oh... I don't think you are,' she smiled. 'Anyway, why should it matter to me?'

'Why shouldn't it?' I asked hopefully.

'You're serious.'

'Maybe,' I shrugged. 'Is the thought of romance with a black man so awful?'

'At one time it would have been,' she said frankly. 'Please don't get upset. We've all inherited attitudes from our past.'

'That's becoming a well used word, "attitudes",' I smiled to take any offence from the words. 'And of course you're right. My father has friends and colleagues of many different persuasions. They were entertained at our home and we were invited to theirs. Yet if I ever took home a girl who wasn't black, they didn't like it. Oh, they never showed it, nor acted in anything other than a polite fashion. But they didn't like it, I know.'

'Were you an only child?' she asked softly.

'No, it was the same with my sister. She chose to go to a red-brick university, where she became very liberated. Like many young people of her acquaintance she went the other way to my parents. She didn't date black boys out of principle.'

'And now?'

'Happily married to a young black lawyer. They have two children and live in a big house in Essex near my parents, who are very pleased. If Elizabeth had married a White they'd have accepted him, and would have loved their grandchildren dearly. But deep inside, they would have been very disappointed. They are the epitome of the English middle class. He belongs to the golf club and she plays bridge and runs fetes. No-one seems to notice their colour any more. But *they* do. They have attitudes, you see.'

She reached across the table and covered my hand with a smaller, paler one.

'I'd love to show you the Cape,' she smiled. 'Anyway, you're not black, you're brown.'

'You're right,' I grinned. 'Tom Jackson. Now, *he's* what I call black.'

We broke into loud peals of laughter, completely out of proportion to the joke.

Yet sometimes it is good to laugh at colour, and attitudes.

Twelve

Naturally enough, John Barnes' articles from the Cape had been mostly political, though none were of a very controversial nature. From his papers I gathered that the one on the ANC finances had been refused by Neville, who didn't want anything that would cast shadows on the future rulers of South Africa. Which is why Barnes had published it locally. Although there was nothing in it that was not already known, the name of a well-known British newsman appended to it gave credibility.

Among the rest of his output were pieces on the wines of the Cape, the old docks development known as the *Waterfront*, the seafood restaurants in Cape Town, and Table Mountain. He'd been quite diverse, had John Barnes. With his writing, as well.

There was also a foolscap sheet with several telephone numbers written on it, and I intended to start ringing around as soon as we got down there.

Marike picked me up at 9 am and we drove in leisurely fashion towards Jan Smuts International Airport. It seemed an age since I'd landed there. We were in no hurry, for our flight didn't leave until noon and we'd promised ourselves a quiet breakfast en route.

'I know the ideal spot,' she said. 'The best pancakes you've ever tasted.'

'Pancakes,' I exclaimed. 'For breakfast? You're thinking of Tom, not me. That's the kind of stuff the Yanks eat. I like good old eggs and bacon myself.'

'Trust me,' she laughed. 'These are savoury pancakes and they fill them with just about anything, including eggs and bacon.'

I was hungry and my mouth began to water at the thought of those savoury pancakes, but fate was about to put breakfast, and my stomach, on hold for a while.

We were passing Joubert Park on our right, on our way to pick up the R24 to the Airport, when I saw Marike glance into the mirror and frown.

'What?' I asked.

'That car behind, the cream Merc, Phillip. It was outside the flat when I picked you up, and has been behind us since we left.'

'Maybe the driver lives in the same road and he's also got a plane to catch at Jan Smuts,' I said reasonably, but I adjusted the rear-view mirror so I could see the car.

It was a cream Mercedes right enough, a big job too. Marike was driving a Honda Ballarde, a nice car but not really in the same class as the Merc. Or so I thought.

'Hold on to your hat,' she said, and slammed down a gear.

Without warning she shot around a battered transit van, geared up again and was off like Nigel Mansel, when he's not being let down by his car that is. Then we came to a red light at the intersection at Twist and Bree, with the traffic running both ways in a continuous stream. Short of suicide she had to stop.

I looked in the mirror again. The Merc was almost on top of us and I noticed the passenger for the first time. Both he and the driver were black. I also noticed the sun glinting off something he held out of the window.

'I, er, think the chap behind has a friend,' I said in what I hoped wasn't a nervous voice. 'And I think he's holding a gun out of the window.'

'He has... and he has,' she said calmly. 'Right both times. Hold tight.'

I thought she was going to leap across the traffic, or at least slide left to join it – South Africa being one of the few sensible countries that still drive on the left – but she did neither.

Instead she threw the Ballarde into reverse and went screaming backwards 'at a rate of knots', as my friend Charlie the Marine would say.

The impact as our back-end hit their front was tremendous. The Merc driver was already hitting the brakes before we struck. Marike and I were slammed backwards, our headrests cushioning the shock. The two behind weren't so fortunate, and the impact threw them forward against the dash.

I was about to climb out and do something heroic, like subdue them while they were stunned and hold them for the police, when Marike took off again. The lights were green this time.

'I think they'll be reluctant to follow us for a while,' I said with forced cheerfulness. 'Who the hell were they, and what were they after?'

'You don't have much imagination, do you?' she shook her head. 'I suppose a discipline like Sociology makes you stick to the facts, but I would have thought in this case the facts spoke for themselves. That car was following us, and the man was poking a gun out of the window. What do *you* think they were after?'

'I suppose they were trying to kill us,' I said reluctantly.

'Not us – *You*.'

I stared at her stupidly.

'I just happen to be with you,' she said. She kept glancing in the rear-view mirror every few seconds. 'I think we'd better have something at the Airport. They might have friends around.'

'You're taking this very calmly,' I muttered. 'As though it was every day someone tried to kill you.'

'In this country we've learned to get used to the possibility of someone trying to kill you. Besides, I've been in a few war zones, remember?'

I remembered, and I was grateful that she'd been the one driving. Along with many other things recently, my chauvinist attitude to women drivers was going through a drastic change. God knows what panic-stricken mistakes I would have made behind the wheel.

I kept my eyes on the rear-view mirror for the rest of the journey to the airport.

Thirteen

We flew *Flitestar*, the internal airline which Marike insisted was the best. She was right. The trip took two and a half hours and they served free drinks the whole time. Although the food looked better than the usual airborne fare, I only picked at it. Despite only drinking coffee in the airport lounge, while I watched Marike tuck into a plateful of breakfast goodies, I still hadn't regained my appetite.

I did take advantage of the free drinks, however. We both did, with the result that we were pretty well sozzled by the time we disembarked at *D.F.Malan* Airport in Cape Town. We sensibly took a taxi instead of picking up a hire car as we'd planned. I thought of her Honda we'd left in the long-stay carpark. I'd been appalled at the damage to the rear, but Marike took it in her stride and shrugged it off with a philosophical remark about being insured. I was impressed.

Marike had booked us into a hotel at Oranjezicht, only minutes from the centre of Cape Town. Originally built around the turn of the century it had been altered and added to several times, and had more of the ambience of an Italian villa than a traditional Dutch residence.

The wide veranda with its arched columns, had sweeping views of Table Mountain and its neighbouring peaks; Lion's Head, Signal Hill, and Devil's Peak. Below, the city stretched out towards the harbour and the sea. We had adjoining rooms above the veranda, and so enjoyed the same views.

By the time we arrived at the hotel I was ravenous. It proved no problem to obtain a late lunch, which was certainly a change from England. Before twelve you get: 'kitchen 'asn't opened yet, luv', and at fifteen minutes to one it's: 'kitchen's closed, mate'. If your stomach refuses to fit in around that hour and three-quarters – tough.

We enjoyed a pleasant lunch, shared more wine, laughed a lot, then decided to turn in for the afternoon. In our separate rooms, of course. I was joined by a giggling Marike a few minutes later, finger to lips in an exaggerated hushing gesture.

Our first session of love-making was not exactly as depicted in the movies – unless between John Candy and the one who played the fat nun in *Sister Act*. It was an inebriated, fumbling attempt at proving how untarnished by worldly values we were, and how much we liked and respected each other. It turned out to be a cross between a soft porn version of Mandingo, and *Mr Bean Feels Randy*. We spent half the time groping each other and the other half giggling, before falling asleep in each other's arms.

We awoke in the same position; naked, entwined, but sober and somewhat embarrassed. It's hard to stay embarrassed in that position for long, and human nature took over.

We made love properly at last and it proved to be good for us both. More than good, perhaps, and much later we parted to get ready for dinner.

And to collect our individual, and thoroughly confused thoughts.

§

I showered, then begin to ring the numbers in Barnes'

briefcase. There were four. The first was a contact Neville had obviously given him, a Cape Town-based Black Rights movement, tokenly disguised from the ANC propaganda machine it really was. I knew this for a fact because Neville had given me the same contact.

The next was a reporter on the Cape Argus newspaper, and the third was no reply. The last number was the one that set bells ringing.

'Hello, this is the home of Kobus Albrecht, Member of Parliament. Who is speaking, please?'

'My name is Phillip O'Brien,' I replied. 'I'd like to speak with Mr Albrecht.'

'May I take a message?' came the smooth voice. It had only the slightest hint of an Afrikaans accent. 'He's not here right now.'

'Tell him it concerns a mutual friend,' I said on impulse. 'John Barnes. I'll ring back later.' I replaced the receiver.

I was already ensconced in the cosy pub/bar when Marike joined me. She wore a green knitted top that matched her eyes, and black harem pants tucked into dark leather Peter Pan bootees. Her hair was loose on her shoulders and she wore a thin gold chain around her neck and big Gypsy earrings. She looked stunning, and more than one male head turned as she moved over to me.

She kissed me on the cheek without hesitation, and the little barman grinned. Before she was even seated, he produced a glass from beneath the counter with a flourish. He had high cheekbones and his skin had a slightly yellowish tinge, handed down from his Khoikhoi forebears.

'What's this?' Marike asked.

'Margarita's,' I lifted my glass. 'Tom introduced me to them, and although the first lot hurt at the time, they sort of grow on you.'

'Ooh, I love them,' she screwed her eyes up and sipped. She rattled off a pile of Afrikaans and the barman's grin became bigger. He replied, but somehow it didn't sound quite the same.

'It's Cape Coloured,' she said. 'Basically Afrikaans, but with their own way of speaking it. I told him these are the best we've ever tasted and he's suitably proud.'

While she was talking I glanced in the mirror and saw a fat couple staring at us. I caught the man's eye and he looked away, but not before I saw the distaste there. It was something I'd have to get used to if I was going to carry on a romance with a blonde. Not only in South Africa either. At least they were open about it here.

'Transvaalers,' Marike said with amusement. 'Though not necessarily. There's a lot of Afrikaners down here. It's surprising how many Brits come to live out here too. In no time they pick up the prejudices of the Afrikaner but without his knowledge of Blacks, and they often treat their servants far worse. Most often it's the working and lower middle classes, who can't believe their luck at the living standards for Whites here.'

'Looks like it's going to change now,' I said. She nodded.

After dinner we went outside onto the veranda, but after a few minutes the cold wind drove us inside to the warm lounge. I was still shivering when I ordered coffee and brandy.

'They call it the *Cape Doctor*,' she laughed softly at my discomfit. 'It's a south-easter which blows from November to March, sometimes reaching speeds of 120 kilometres an hour. It lulls in the morning, and has its peaks of fury in the afternoon.'

'Thanks,' I muttered. 'Now she tells me.'

'Well, it can be tiresome, and during the summer Cape Town can be one of the three windiest places on earth, but it does have its advantages. It makes the city's atmosphere one of the healthiest in the world, because the *Doctor* blows away insects, dust, and other kinds of pollution.'

'You sound like a tourist blurb,' I gave a mock

frown. 'I take it there *are* some days when we can actually get down to the sea?'

'Oh, yes. The *Doctor* doesn't blow *all* the time. But as for the sea... well, it depends what side you go.'

'What side?' I was becoming increasingly suspicious of this place, despite the wonderful views. 'What side of what?'

'The Cape is where two oceans meet, remember?' She was enjoying this, I could tell. 'The Atlantic is on the west coast, and even in summer the temperature is only about 15°C.'

'And the east coast?'

'The Indian Ocean is warmer, but still cold to anyone used to swimming in Durban. Shouldn't be a problem to you, though. You Poms are used to cold water.'

'Poms like me wouldn't dream of swimming in the sea around Britain at any time of the year,' I said with feeling. 'I'm not too sure about this *Fairest Cape.*'

'Wait till the morning,' she laughed. 'With a bit of luck the tablecloth will be laid.'

She didn't elaborate, as the coffee and brandy arrived providing a lull in the conversation. After that we talked about small, inconsequential things from the past. I told her I'd never married because of the pressures of my work, and the inevitable travelling of a documentary film-maker. She listened intently and nodded politely, but I could tell she didn't believe a word. I was about to switch the personal stuff onto her when she reminded me of the call I wanted to make. I'd told her about Albrecht earlier but she'd passed no comment at the time.

It was nine-thirty and the same coldly polite voice answered. I insisted on speaking to Kobus Albrecht personally, yet still received firmly evasive chat.

'Perhaps you could be more explicit, Mr O'Brien,' the distant voice made it sound like a command. I hate commands.

'I could, but I don't intend to,' I brought frigidity into my own voice. 'I told you this morning it was about

92

a man named John Barnes. As he is now dead, and I have reason to believe he was acquainted with Mr Albrecht, I would have thought your employer might have been interested, but obviously not. In which case I shall simply pass on the information to the police, and I'll bid you good night.'

There was a pause, a very slight pause, then another voice came on the line. He must have been listening on an extension, for there was no time to have passed on what I'd said.

'I am Kobus Albrecht,' he said in a heavy accent. 'You are Irish, Mr O'Brien?'

'Black Irish, Mr Albrecht,' I smiled into the phone. 'From way back. Actually I'm as English as Yorkshire pud or faggots.'

'Faggots?' the voice took on a new tone, one I couldn't recognise at first.

'It's a dish made from brains and stuff,' I replied curiously. 'Equally it can be a bundle of sticks that they used in the old bread ovens. What did you think I was...?'

The penny dropped, and I wondered why the family brain cell wasn't functioning today.

'I think we must meet, *meneer*' he said, and that was that. His minion came back on the line and gave me the address, with the instruction that 11 o'clock the next morning would be suitable. He made it sound like a Presidential order and an audience with the Pope at the same time.

I returned to the lounge and regaled Marike with the highlights of the call.

'You took a chance,' she raised an eyebrow charmingly. 'You have no idea who Albrecht is, I suppose?'

'Apart from a Member of Parliament, no,' I finished my brandy and raised my hand to the barman.

'He's been an MP in the National Party for as long as I can remember. There was a time he was very much flavour of the month and served a few terms in the Cabinet; Minister for this and that. His highest

93

achievement was Law and Order Minister, which was many years ago and there was very little justice in his ministry during that time.'

She paused while the little barman placed two more brandies in front of us, 'During his office deaths in custody rose alarmingly, and any attempts to investigate were hindered so much that they could get nowhere. In Jo'burg Police HQ there's a fourth floor interview room. Black prisoners had a tendency of leaping out of the window almost daily. I know because I was a crime reporter at the time.'

'And Albrecht lost his job over it?'

'Hardly,' she picked up the fresh brandy. 'He only lost favour when de Klerk arrived. FW began to weed out the hard right, knowing what his future plans were, and aware of the opposition he would get when they were known. Albrecht, however, still controls the powerful Afrikaner lobby, and can't be ignored entirely.'

'Perhaps Barnes had something on him,' I murmured. 'His reaction to the word *faggots*. He thought I was having a go at him. If he was gay, would it make any difference to his standing?'

'Not with the Blacks or Coloureds,' she chuckled. 'But with the Afrikaners he'd be finished. It might be fashionable to be gay in Britain and America, but the Boer still sees it as being against the will of God.'

'It does seem to have got out of hand,' I admitted. 'Straight people are almost apologising for not being gay. Like militant Blacks, they get people's backs up and it just makes them resentful. Now whether or not Albrecht is gay, can you think of any reason for him to want John Barnes dead?'

'None at all,' she shook her head, causing the blonde hair to swirl around her neck. 'No use guessing until we see him.'

'We? There's no *we* about it,' I frowned. 'I'm going there on my own, young lady, so...'

'Blow it out of your ear,' she said crudely. 'I've always wanted to meet the bigoted bastard. And talking of wasting time, is it too early to go to bed yet?'

It wasn't, and we did, though I was still arguing about her accompanying me the next day. Until we got to her door, then all interest in argument fell away like leaves in autumn as a poet or a forty-year old black man – who thought he was in love – might say.

Fourteen

She was right about the tablecloth. We woke up to it. The crowning glory of Table Mountain was the strangely neat cap of cloud which unrolled across the flat summit and draped itself over the edges in a tidy, almost straight, line. The tablecloth.

I made coffee from the courtesy supply by the jug, and we stood in dressing gowns by the window, drinking and gazing up at the mountain. In precise reportage, Marike explained the reasons why there was cloud on the mountain, yet nowhere else in the sky.

It begins over the sea far to the south. Whirling belts of high pressure, which girdle the earth at certain latitudes, throw off tongues of air that reach up to the tip of Africa. When they hit the mountains along the coast, this air is forced to change direction, and picking up speed, it searches for a way through the mountain barricade. It finds a gap, and rushes around Cape Hangklip, swirling across the waters of False Bay, and collecting moisture on the way.

When it reaches the shores of False Bay, the wind collides with the mountains of the Cape peninsula and is forced to rise. Soon it reaches the cooler altitudes of the mountain tops, where it condenses into thick white clouds. Table Mountain is just the right shape and in just the right place to arrange these clouds in a most unusual way. Being the highest point of the range it catches the bulk of the clouds, which roll across the flat summit and pour over the edges to be abruptly dissolved in the warmer air of a lower altitude. Thus creating the scenic wonder of the famous tablecloth.

'I'm gobsmacked,' I said in Liverpudlian, and I was.

'You see,' she tossed her head and laughed. 'The nasty old *Cape Doctor* has his good points. He leaves the air invigoratingly clean and clear; he drives warm water into False Bay from the Mozambique-Agulhas Current off the east coat; and best of all he creates the tablecloth.'

I raised my empty cup to the *Cape Doctor* in a mocking fashion and was immediately punished for it, as a small hand disappeared beneath my dressing gown. I learned in physics that for every action there's a reaction, and I reacted as expected. It was back to bed for a while.

'It's a good match, isn't it?' Marike murmured later.

At first I thought she was referring to the mountain and its cloud, which we could see from the bed. Then I saw she was looking down at our naked bodies, limbs entwined around each other. Black and white, but not really. It was a lot closer than that, for I was as brown as a deeply tanned white man, and she was a light copper from the first effects of the summer sun. But the soft delicate hairs on her arms were golden, as was the triangle of her womanhood.

'A good match,' I agreed. For it was.

Breakfast was quiet and intimate, and although there were several other people in the dining room, it was as though we were on our own. The waiters were discreet, unobtrusive and extremely polite, and not for the first time I wished their opposite numbers in Britain could see them perform their duties. They could learn a lot.

97

Albrecht lived in Hout Bay, a beautiful beach and fishing harbour overlooked by towering mountains. Its entrance is guarded by the Sentinel, a peak also known as the Hangberg. It was remote and picturesque, yet the trip itself would take only 20 minutes from Oranjezicht if we went through Kloof Nek. Instead we left earlier and went around the back of the mountain, keeping it to our right and took the Ou Kaapse Weg through the Silvermine nature reserve.

We joined Chapman's Peak Drive, which went around the Peak itself, and on our left was a sheer drop into the Atlantic. To our right was the tail end of the range that began with Table Mountain, then became the glowering peaks of the Twelve Apostles. A little further on and I looked across the sweep of Hout Bay, where I could see the 1000ft high Sentinel looming over the sheltered harbour, with its colourful fishing boats bobbing on their moorings. I think it must be one of the world's most spectacular scenic drives, even though I've been from one end of the Côte d'Azur to the other.

We passed through the village filled with quaint shops and restaurants, and headed up into the hills beyond. The MP's residence stood alone behind a small stand of trees.

'Hout Bay is the Anglicized version of *Houtbaai*, which means *wood bay*,' Marike explained as we turned up a winding drive across the hillside. 'It was named in the 17th century because the bay was filled with trees, and the ships would put in here to replace their timbers. Now, those we've just passed are the only ones left. Sad.'

An armed guard stood behind a high entrance gate, itself dwarfed by taller walls that ran away to right and left. I called out my name and a few moments later the wide gate slid smoothly open.

We drove through and the guard merely stared as I waved a hand. The drive had a broad strip of neatly cut buffalo grass on either side, with indigenous plants growing up to its edge. About five hundred yards from the gate we came to the house itself. A great column of cement and glass rose steeply above us, resting on huge pillars of reinforced concrete. The base was open at the front but further back was a line of garaging, with two Mercedes and a 4 wheel drive twin cab parked in front.

Marike drove under the house and stopped between the Mercs. As we climbed out of the car a man appeared from a doorway adjacent to the garages. He was short and dapper, with a neatly parted head of obviously dyed hair. He was about my age.

He stared at us for a moment, as though unable to grasp the information his eyes were conveying to his brain. Where he had expected to see a solitary white man with an Irish name, he was now confronted with a black man and a blonde woman.

'Mr O'Brien? I'm Gerrit van Rensberg, Mr Albrecht's personal assistant.'

I introduced Marike and he shook hands with her. He did not extend the same courtesy to me, and I was left in no doubt where things stood with van Rensberg. He led us to the door he'd emerged from and to my surprise it was a lift. He said nothing on the ride up, but stood with hands folded over his crotch and gazed at the floor indicator with single-minded fascination.

From B for basement it went through 1 to 5 then stopped at R, and we stepped out onto the roof.

The view was magnificent, with the whole of the bay opening up across our front. Behind us the mountains rose steep and green until the last sections were sheer grey rock.

Half of the rooftop was swimming pool, and the rest paid homage to outdoor living. A brick barbecue, or *braai*, looked big enough to cook for a regiment, and the amount of seating would have accommodated them all. Alongside the pool was a jacuzzi into which a soccer team would have fitted comfortably. Maybe they did, I thought nastily.

Sprawled on one of the many loungers around the pool was Kobus Albrecht, in the flesh. He was about 60 years of age, but a well preserved 60. His hair was silver and cut short with a neat parting on the left. Eating and drinking were obviously pleasures he took care with, for although the flesh was sagging here and there, he had no discernible gut. The only feature that detracted from the all-over appearance was his eyes. They were set unusually wide apart, giving an impression of in-breeding.

When he saw me his eyes narrowed, but only for a moment. The politician in him came to the fore and he rose with some difficulty.

'Mr O'Brien,' he said in a voice that was strangely soft, yet guttural at the same time. He took my hand without hesitation, and instead of the strong grip I expected it was gentle enough to be almost a caress. 'I thought you'd be alone.'

It was not accusative, yet I gained the impression I'd been reprimanded in some way. I apologised, though I didn't know why, and introduced Marike Geldenhuys.

'*Goeie môre, meneer*' she said politely. I noticed he merely touched her hand, whereas he'd lingered over mine.

He invited us to sit down and led us to a table and chairs beneath a sun umbrella. He sent his PA to call one of the servants and while we waited he exchanged a few sentences with Marike in Afrikaans. A young black man appeared and Albrecht barked an order at him.

'I hope some good Cape wine will be all right, but please order something else if you prefer.' Although the words were polite, the tone was such that one did not argue with. We both murmured something about the wisdom of his choice.

While we waited for the wine we spent the time in small talk. At least Albrecht did.

'How long have you been here, Mr O'Brien?' he asked.

100

'Only a couple of weeks,' I replied.

'So, what do you think of the new free society of South Africa?'

'It depends how free your particular society is at the moment,' I said carefully. 'Obviously there are great differences here.'

'Of course,' he agreed, in a way which might have been considered salubrious if his accent had not got in the way. 'Just as in your country there are great differences. You have many troublemakers among your minority groups. Muslims, Pakistanis, Sikhs, West Indians, African Blacks from Nigeria, Uganda and the like. We read all the time about their attempts to change the basic culture of Britain, and incredible as it sounds they appear to be succeeding. Where do you originate from, Mr O'Brien?'

There was a mocking note in his voice that I took offence to, and I ignored Marike's warning glance from across the table.

'Strangely enough, Mr Albrecht,' I repeated myself for the second time in a few days. 'I was born in Britain, as was my father, his father before him, and a line that goes back to 1700 and something. I imagine they emigrated from Africa about the same time that your people were coming out here. Or am I a few dates out?'

'No,' he smiled but only with his lips, for the eyes remained humourless. 'I think your dates are probably correct. We have both done well from our forefathers chosen countries it seems.'

'Except mine never had a choice,' I said coldly. 'My ancestors did not arrive in their new country in a Dutch East Indiaman, but a slaving ship.'

At that moment the young black man returned, complete with starched white coat and a tray with a wine cooler and glasses. Whatever reply Albrecht was preparing remained unsaid. The servant poured wine into four glasses, which he placed before us and discreetly withdrew.

I put my nose to the glass and sipped slowly, rolling it around my palate and letting it slide down my throat. I was aware that Albrecht was watching me with some amusement. Which is why I was performing of course.

'What do you think of our wine, Mr O'Brien? I take it you are a wine drinker?'

'It's excellent,' I said. 'A varietal wine with a delicate bouquet and characteristic Riesling flavour. I assume it is a certified Wine of Origin?'

'Of course,' he inclined his well-groomed head. 'It's a Nederburg, and comes from Klein Drakenstein in the Paarl Area, named after Commissioner-General Nederburg of the Dutch East India Company. The wine-making was started in 1937 by a German named Johann Graue and they produce some of our finest wines.

'What do you think of the flavour?'

It was a trick question – I sniffed it and put the glass down. 'As I said, it has the characteristic Riesling flavour, and a nice bouquet.'

'You didn't taste it,' Marike said.

'No,' I looked at Albrecht.

'In the strict scientific sense taste can only refer to impressions received via the taste buds of the mouth and these are restricted to sour, sweet, bitter and salty. Flavours, on the other hand, are all smell sensations and therefore dependent on the nose.'

'Well said, Mr O'Brien,' our genial host raised his glass in acknowledgement. 'You appear to know about wine.'

'I should do,' I replied with acerbity. 'I've been used to drinking wine with my meals since I was young. As my father is something of a wine buff I grew up with it.'

Albrecht was smiling, but whether he was really amused at the expounding about wine I didn't know. His PA, van Rensberg, didn't bother to smile. He *certainly* wasn't amused. I wondered what it would take to amuse him. He should sue God or his parents for not giving him a sense of humour, I thought.

'What did your father do?' Albrecht asked, rather rudely.

'He *is* a medical doctor, and I have an honours degree in sociology. I support Everton Football Club and my favourite colour is green. Anything else you'd like to know?'

I looked into Marike's green eyes when I said it and she held a hand to her mouth to suppress a giggle. She giggled a lot and I found it endearing. Van Rensberg obviously didn't.

'What is your purpose in coming here, Mr O'Brien?' He demanded. 'Are you a journalist?'

'No, but you're close. John Barnes was, and I'm investigating his death.' *Investigating* sounded more upmarket than *nosing around for a friend*. 'I take it you knew of his death, Mr Albrecht?'

'I read about it in the newspaper,' he replied, and watched me over the top of his glass as he drank. 'Terrible thing to happen to a visitor to our country. Ritual murder, wasn't it? For *muti* or something?'

'No, it wasn't a *muti* murder,' I stared back at him. He flicked his eyes at his personal assistant, but van Rensberg gave no acknowledgement. Someone to watch, I thought, our Mr van Rensberg. 'I spoke to someone who knows how these things are done, and there are several anomalies which rule it out. It was, of course, meant to *look* like such.'

'Articles, interviews,' he shrugged. 'They don't have to be political to upset people here these days, Mr O'Brien. Didn't he do some stuff on the Transvaal, cover a rally or something?'

You know he did, you fat white pig, I thought tightly. I wondered how much else he knew.

'How well did you know John Barnes?'

'Not well, at all. He interviewed me for a political article he was writing. A few months ago wasn't it, Gerrit?'

The dyed blond head inclined slightly. 'A few months ago, yes, Kobus.'

'Did you ever see him socially, Mr Albrecht?' Marike had said little since we'd arrived, and they looked at her in surprise.

'No, not at all. The interview was held here in my own home, and lasted about two hours. I never saw Mr Barnes again.'

'What did he question you on? Was it all politics?' Marike was much better at this than I was. I was too busy reacting to real or imagined slights, but she was asking the right things.

'Of course,' Albrecht was getting rather tired of us now, but managing to keep his cool quite well. 'He wanted to know what I thought of the future of my party after the elections. How many seats we'd make, how we'd get on with the other parties, etcetera'

'If it wasn't ritual, nor the work of right wing Afrikaners, who do *you* think might have had reasons to kill a visiting journalist, Mr Albrecht?' She was *good*.

Again that quick glance at van Rensberg, and if it was for support, he got it.

'Mr Albrecht met him just the one time, as he told you,' he said. 'So he could hardly be expected to form an opinion as to his death, Miss Geldenhuys.'

'I thought as a politician he might have an idea what kind of enquiries could result in a person turning up dead,' she said reasonably, not at all intimidated by van Rensberg.

Nothing I can think of, Miss Geldenhuys,' the wide-set eyes screwed in concentration. 'In these trying times anything could set someone off. Any group that suspected a slight, perhaps.'

I was the only one facing towards the mountains, the others sitting in a half circle with a view out across the bay, so it was only I who saw the young servant at the door leading down to the house. He was making some gesture with his hand that I couldn't make out.

I enquired where the toilet was and excused

myself. As I descended the short flight of stairs to the next level, the man came out of a corridor from the left.

'Sir. Mr Barnes. You were a friend of his?' he asked in a soft voice. Soft to the point of being effeminate. I nodded, wondering what it was all about.

'I knew Mr Barnes... he was a nice man. There is a club, in Long Street, it is called The Closet. Mr Barnes used to go there with Mr Albrecht. They...'

The door opened and closed above us and we heard footsteps coming down the stairs.

'I cannot speak here, sir. Please meet me in town, I am off tonight. There is a new English pub opened in Green Market Square... ten o'clock. Please...'

He disappeared and I climbed back up the stairs.

'Mr van Rensberg,' I said in mock surprise. 'Don't you know it is unlucky to cross on the stairs?'

He was on the step above me yet still his head wasn't quite level with mine. Instead of daunting him, however, it seemed to make him believe it was his natural height.

'I think it would be wise if you went now, Mr O'Brien,' his voice would have given an Eskimo the chills. 'Mr Albrecht likes to nap after lunch.'

Obviously we weren't invited to stay for lunch, though it didn't come as a surprise.

'Alone?' I kept a straight face. 'You're very thoughtful on his behalf. It must be very lucrative.'

'The job has its own rewards,' he said primly.

'I don't suppose you can tell me anything more about John Barnes, just between the two of us. I'm very discreet, and I'm not a newspaperman.'

'No, but your lady friend is,' he replied. 'Not that I could help you, anyway. This way please, Mr O'Brien.'

He led the way to the roof, where we took our leave of Kobus Albrecht. I thought there was a slight relief in his voice as we made our farewells. Again that little squeeze as we shook hands. Whatever prejudices the overweight MP and his PA might share, shaking hands with a black man wasn't one of them.

Fifteen

We took the short route back through Kloof Nek. As we passed Llandudno Bay I laughed at the way Marike said the name. I gave it the correct Welsh pronunciation of 'Klan-did-no', trying to make up for the Afrikaans words I kept getting wrong.

We stopped at Camp's Bay for lunch, a small restaurant with tables and umbrellas on the pavement in the Mediterranean style. Marike suggested a bottle of Gracás, an imported Portugese wine that was probably the cheapest and best value around. I ordered snails, which Marike screwed up her nose at, calling me a peasant, and she had mushrooms with melted Stilton.

We shared pizza and Greek salad, and another bottle of Gracas seemed the sensible thing to do.

Irish coffee followed the wine, and by the time we arrived back at the hotel we were again in a happily glowing state. We showered together in her room and tumbled into bed. It was wonderful, for we were still discovering the mysteries of each other; not just our bodies, but our minds.

Only when we woke at seven thirty, showered again and drank the coffee Marike made, did we talk about meeting Albrecht's servant.

'It could be a trap,' she murmured, holding her cup in both hands and gazing wisely over the rim.

'I doubt it,' I smiled. 'If Albrecht wanted to do us harm he could have arranged it in advance and placed someone on the way back along the coast. A sniper's bullet in a front tyre could have caused a nasty accident. Like sending us over the cliff.'

'He didn't know which way we'd go back.'

'He didn't have to. He could have put a man on both roads.'

'True,' she wrinkled her nose. 'So what do *you* think he wants, O clever one?'

'Haven't a clue,' I said honestly. 'Let's not waste time trying to work it out. Get dressed and we'll go somewhere different.'

If there's one thing guaranteed to motivate a woman, it's to promise her a surprise. Sit back and watch the reaction. By eight o'clock we were ready to go. We had a drink in the hotel bar, making our little barman's day by ordering Margaritas.

We walked into the Japanese restaurant in Long Street at eight thirty. It was done out as it would be in Japan and Marike was impressed. Suspicious, but impressed.

'I've never eaten Japanese food,' she confessed, while we were waiting to be shown to a table.

'You've had Chinese, haven't you?' I asked.

'Well, yes...'

'This is nothing like Chinese,' I grinned. 'It's a sushi bar. You can sit at the counter and gobble and go, or take one of the high Western tables over there, *or* go to the back, take your shoes off and fold your legs under one of those low jobs. You've got it all here, from fast food to decadent lounging.'

She said the thought of raw fish made her squirm, but after we'd shared a jug of warm saki, and the waitress had sworn a sacred oath that the fish was fresh that very day, she tried some. There was salmon, tuna and yellowtail, and the mustard-based sauce was delicious.

Of course Marike enjoyed it, and we ordered a few

more dishes and another jug of saki. I was used to the strong rice wine and warned Marike about its nasty habit of creeping up on one. We wanted to be reasonably alert for ten o'clock.

At twenty-minutes to, we strolled around the corner from the sushi bar and down to Green Market Square. During the day it was filled with market stalls, but in the evening there were various coloured musicians scattered around, watched by people from hotel patios, enjoying their after-dinner coffee. We strolled past one group with heavily blackened faces and brightly coloured outfits.

'They're getting ready for the Coon Carnival. It's a traditional New Year event in the Cape,' Marike said.

'You mean the Coloureds are taking the mickey out of the Blacks?' I asked in astonishment.

'It does seem like that I suppose,' she laughed. 'It sprung from thanksgiving celebrations when the slaves were liberated, and its origins are in the Bo-Kaap, where the Cape Malays live. There were probably bands of coloured musicians around at that time, but the present troupes came from a baker named Cole at the end of the last century. He gave his coloured workers costumes and top-hats to advertise his bread and it has carried on from there.'

I was watching a fiddler and a banjo player hammering away on 'Duelling Banjos' from *Deliverance*, and they were good – at least as far as my unmelodic ears could tell.

'They have violins, banjos, guitars and tambourines, and march along like soldiers behind a fantastic drum-major, then the music starts and they begin dancing and playing their own versions.

'It's a sight to see, and the names too. Cherry Pickers, Mississipi Darkies, Diamond Eyes, Kentucky Victory Coons... some of them are wonderful.'

'Sounds like a New Orleans funeral. I visited there once.'

She nodded. 'The comparison has been made

before. Over the years the Malay and Hottentot mix has been added to by Whites, and as you can see, some of the Coloureds are pretty light skinned. I don't know why, but there isn't a lot of intermarriage with the Blacks.'

I was still pondering the idea of a coloured person blackening his face and performing a Nigger Minstrel show, when we entered the 'traditional' Irish pub on the corner of the main hotel. It had green tartan everywhere; on the walls, the carpets, even the short skirts of the young waitresses. I was about to introduce myself as a member of the Black Watch and ask where our tartan was, but thought better of it.

They had a different sense of humour out here.

We ordered drinks and sat in a corner which had views of both doors. By ten-thirty the servant lad hadn't made an appearance. I was wondering what our next move should be, when Marike took the initiative away from me.

'Let's give him another five minutes,' she said, breaking into my thoughts again. 'I've spent a lot of hours waiting for informants in bars. If he doesn't show we can always find that club he mentioned.'

I agreed and sipped my drink with a nonchalence I didn't feel. I was worried for that poor boy, and it didn't help that Rensberg's sour-looking face kept coming into my field of vision.

'Good idea,' I said, and five minutes later we were on our way back to Long Street. I got the location from one of the barmaids, who gave me a funny look along with the address.

'Must be a place where gays hang out,' I said, with my usual mastery of the understatement.

§

'*You* can come in, dear, but not your nanny,' the blimp on the door told us in a high-pitched voice. He looked, and sounded, like a eunuch. Not that I've ever actually

109

seen one, but I had read the Arabian Nights. He was huge, with hair tied back in a ponytail and dressed in a collarless white shirt with enormous frills on the cuffs. His tight black pants were literally bursting at the seams, and he had outsized golden pumps on his outsized feet. He dripped gold; chains, bracelets, rings.

'I'll wait for you. Look after yourself, dear,' Marike smiled sweetly. 'I'll interview Demis Roussos here to pass the time. We'll talk about fashion.'

She was wearing a white blouse tucked into green slacks, emphasising her figure to perfection, and the eunuch was sighing with envy.

It cost R50 to get through the door, and the interior appeared to be in total darkness after the street lights outside. A single spotlight shot out and hit me full in the face, causing me to blink and hold a hand up to shade it. I heard various muttering and suggestions from close by and then the light was gone and wall sconces around the room came on. Apparently it was standard practice to illuminate newcomers to the club so the older hands could get a good perv.

A round bar stood in the centre, and the walls were lined with booths, each with a heavy red curtain that could be pulled across for complete privacy. What went on behind them I shuddered to think. Two round dance floors matched the bar on either side and the rest of the space was filled with cosy little tables with candles on. The place was fairly well patronised for such an early time of the evening, and most of the bar-stools had bottoms on them.

I moved over to the bar and ordered a whisky and soda. The barman was White and wore a blue Paisley shirt with gold lamè shorts. His long blond hair had sequins, and was probably a wig. He also wore far too much make-up, but as his sleeves were rolled above tattooed arms I refrained from enlightening him. Or her. Whatever. It wasn't the tattoos that bothered me, as much as the bulging biceps they were attached to.

'Have one yourself,' I invited generously, and he

poured himself a small Coke and charged me five rand for it. 'Tell me, has Kobus come in yet? Kobus Albrecht?'

'No,' he said in a surprisingly normal voice. He didn't mince either, I noticed, nor lisp or ponce around as you would expect. He simply dressed in drag. 'He usually comes in later, about midnight. With his lady-in-waiting.'

'Gerrit?' I guessed.

'That's right, nasty piece of work,' he frowned. 'Perverted little arsehole if you ask me.'

I managed to keep a straight face at the unfortunate choice of words, but I thought he was probably right.'

'Do you remember him coming in a few months ago, with a young Black chap?'

'You're a Pommie, aren't you?' he asked, ignoring the question.

'That's right,' I nodded. 'Same as John Barnes... the young Black man I just asked you about?'

He still didn't get the message, or didn't want to, and I turned to the man on my right. He'd been taking a strong interest in our conversation and it was time he made a contribution.

'Do *you* know who I'm talking about?'

'Oh, yes,' he nodded a jet black wig that contrasted oddly with his extremely old face. 'I remember. Good-looking boy. I'm into good-looking Black boys, you know. Like yourself.'

Yes, you old shirt-lifter, I thought, I suppose I would look like a boy to you.

'Thank you,' I smiled, as though I'd been paid a compliment. 'Did they come in together often?'

'Oh, yes. It was quite a little thing they had going for a while. They were in here most nights, and I gathered his...'

'That's enough, Reggie,' the barman said, though not unkindly. 'You know we don't discuss the customers in here.'

111

'Surely the customers can talk between themselves?' I asked sharply.

'Sure,' he shrugged. 'Except Reggie isn't a customer. He plays the piano over there, and he's just about to begin. You ask a lot of questions, friend.'

'I don't get many answers though.'

'Why do I get the feeling you're a reporter?' the barman said evenly, and I saw him glance over my shoulder.

Behind me stood the blimp doorman, accompanied by a much shorter but more muscular man.

'I just knew you were trouble, love,' the eunuch said. 'You and the blonde tart, you work for some newspaper, right? And you're spying on our customers.'

'Not customers, just customer. Albrecht. The man he was seen with here is dead, and I think the police might have some enquiries to make when they find out.'

It was the wrong thing to say. I found that out as soon as I'd said it. Mind you, it always seemed to work in the movies...

'Don't threaten us, you black sod,' the barman said in that matter-of-fact tone of his. 'Not in my own place.' For *Barman* now read *Owner*. 'Throw him out.'

They did. At least they got as far as the door. I had no intention of causing trouble, but I hadn't let Marike know that.

We were in a line, the blimp/eunuch in front and the muscular dwarf behind. As we passed the desk a blonde wildcat emerged from the shadows and attacked the poor fat man. She kicked him in the side of the knee, twisting her foot in some peculiar fashion so that the edge took him on the joint and made him squeal. The sound he made was very much like that of a pig.

I had no choice after that. As Marike brought a vicious knee into the side of his face, I cupped my left hand over my right fist and drove my elbow back into the face of the man behind me.

As he collapsed, I stepped over the equally limp

form of the blimp who was now lying down in front of me.

Marike had the nerve to laugh, and grabbed my hand as we went out of the door together and ran down the street, with her giggling and me trying not to have a nervous breakdown. As soon as we were around a corner somewhere, and had slowed down, I went into my indignant phase.

'Why the hell did you do that,' I hissed. 'I was only being escorted out. They weren't going to beat me up or anything.'

'You don't know that for a fact,' she sniffed. 'And neither did I. Better safe than sorry.'

'My mother used to say that – all the time.'

'What?'

'Better safe than sorry,' I muttered. 'What did you do to the eunuch back there? Was it some kind of karate or what?'

'Or what,' she smirked. 'A girl has to know how to defend herself in the world today. Especially the places my work sends me to. I took lessons.'

'A pity you couldn't have passed them on,' I told her.

'Why? You did alright back there. The elbow in the face was a fancy piece of work.'

'I didn't mean me,' I said soberly. 'I meant the poor sod who works for Albrecht and was going to meet us in the pub.'

'Oh, dear. I'd forgotten about him.'

'I hadn't. There's only one reason springs to mind why he failed to turned up. They got to him first.'

Sixteen

We caught a taxi back to Oranjesicht and sat in the bar drinking Irish coffees while we went over what we had so far. Personally I thought we were wasting our efforts and it was time to call it a day.

'Rubbish,' she said firmly. 'We're on to something here, I can feel it in my journalist's blood...'

'Which is black as printer's ink,' I mumbled.

'Which *is* printer's ink,' she corrected. 'Barnes had a homosexual relationship with Albrecht, who is a right-wing Member of Parliament and needs the Afrikaner vote to keep his job. If it gets out that he's gay they won't like it very much, and if they find out that he's been sleeping with a *Black* man, he'll be history. Both motives for murder.'

'Mmm, I don't think it's as easy as that,' I finished my coffee and held a hand up for two more. Like most Coloureds, the little barman had an English name, and he was called Charlie Williams. Which had made me smile because I remembered a British comedian with the same name. He had a pronounced Yorkshire accent and was one of the first Black entertainers in Britain.

'Blackmail.' I said.

'Blackmail?'

'Blackmail. If someone was putting the black on Albrecht, he wouldn't be too... what's the matter?'

She'd suddenly gone into a paroxysm of mirth and my puzzled look didn't help much.

'I'm sorry,' she spluttered. 'But "putting the black on", you must have spent an awful lot of time watching old American movies.'

'As a matter of fact I did,' I said huffily. 'But it happens to fit in with what I was saying, *If* I might be allowed to continue.'

She nodded, hand over mouth and big eyes shining with tears.

'If it was Barnes doing the blackmail, then surely it would be the best motive for murder so far.'

That shut her up, and we were both quiet for a while, mulling over what was in our minds. For my part the blackmail theory made it even more sensible to cut and run. If I was right then it could be argued that Barnes had got what he deserved. What more could we do now, anyway? Our reasons for suspecting Albrecht – or his little pal Gerrit – of being involved were not proof, nor were they evidence.

So what difference could we make if we went on? John Barnes was dead, and even if he'd been a close friend it still wouldn't bring him back no matter what we did. I also had a book to write, I reminded myself unneccessarily.

I was about to mention all this to the lovely girl sitting next to me, but she looked up and smiled, and I didn't have the heart to say anything. I knew she could smell a story and wouldn't let go until she had it.

We said good-night to Charlie and went upstairs. I went to brush my teeth in my own room before joining her and saw the envelope as soon as I opened the door. It was a plain white envelope with my name printed rather crudely on the front.

Inside was a photo of a man. It was the black servant from Albrecht's house, the one we should have met earlier. I'd been right about his failure to turn up. He was dead. He was on his back and the eyes were open and staring in such a way that you knew he was no longer with us. Somehow being right was less than gratifying.

There was no note in the envelope. There was no need. The message was in the photo.

§

It was another couple of hours before we went to bed that night. Marike shivered when I showed her the photo, and said nothing for a while.

'I think it could be bigger than we thought,' she said finally. 'Maybe we should go to the police.'

'You don't mean that?' I frowned.

'No, I don't suppose I do. But this does point the finger firmly at Albrecht now, doesn't it?'

'Yes, it does,' I agreed. 'Maybe a bit too firmly. Come on, let's sleep on it.'

'If that's what you really want to do,' she gave an exaggerated sigh. 'What time shall I set the alarm for?'

'Late. Very late. Now come here, and convince me we're doing the right thing carrying on with this.'

'You know we're doing the right thing,' she said softly. 'John Barnes might have been homosexual but he doesn't sound like a blackmailer. And he *is* one of your people, after all.'

'What's one of my people?' I asked curiously.

'A Black Englishman. Surely you're not going to let these *kaffir*-bashers get away with it?'

She was indulging in some gentle goading but she was right.

'Where a man has once taken up his stand, either because it seems best to him or in obedience to his orders, there I believe he is bound to remain and face the danger, taking no account of death or anything else before dishonour.'

'Machiavelli,' she said triumphantly. 'From *The Prince*.'

'Wrong,' I said smugly. 'They're the words of Socrates, written by Plato after his death. What it

116

means is that I intend to carry on, if for no other reason than the photograph. It was a warning for us to back off, and I don't like being threatened.'

'Well, didn't *they* make a mistake?' she cocked her head to one side. 'Tomorrow we take a break and I'm going to show you Table Mountain close up.'

'Do we have to climb it?' I gave an exaggerated groan.

'If you really want to, but it might be easier to take the cable car. We can have lunch in the tea-room up there, wander around a bit, and have sundowners on the balcony. How does that sound?'

'Sounds great, but let me tell you what sounds better right now...'

I pushed her onto the bed and whispered what I had in mind. There was no argument.

Seventeen

Marike had ignored my suggestion about the alarm and we were up very early the next morning; washed, dressed, breakfasted, and waiting for the first car going up the mountain. The lower cableway station was not far from our hotel, for which I was very grateful at that hour.

Table Mountain is a vast block of sandstone 1,086 metres high, and rising on its northern face as a sheer precipice more than 3 kilometres long. From a distance it appears to be unbroken, but closer inspection reveals a deep cleft, Platteklip Gorge, splitting it from base to summit.

The mountain is visible at times as far as 200 kilometres out to sea, and made the anchorage of Table Bay easy to find, with the offer of shelter, drinking water, and produce from the farms nestling at its feet. The first recorded ascent was in 1503 by Antonio de Saldanha, a Spanish admiral, who struggled up Platteklip Gorge to prove his incompetent pilot a liar by sighting False Bay.

But no amount of facts and figures about the mountain could prepare you for the reality of it. There were now more than 350 routes to the summit, ranging from easy scrambles to dangerous climbs. Fortunately we were taking the easiest way. The aerial cableway, built in 1929, had never had an accident, which was nice to know but did nothing for my fear of heights.

There were about 20 people in front of us, and I assumed we'd be in the second or third car, but to my nervous surprise we were in the first.

'Didn't I mention they take 28 passengers?' Marike grinned.

The trip itself took only six minutes, but I wasted three of them gazing fixedly at the sheer rock wall as we rose towards it. When Marike finally dragged me around by the arm, I had to admit it was worth it.

The city of Cape Town and Table Bay were spread out below. To our left, connected to the mountain by Kloof Nek, Lion's Head stood silhouetted against the blue waters of False Bay, and to the right I could see the saddle between Devil's Peak and its minor feature beyond. I was just beginning to enjoy it when the ride was over, and I determined to make the descent with my back to the cliff.

Except someone had other ideas about that.

We meandered up the stairway from the car and emerged on the edge of the most stunning view I've ever seen. To the south is the Cape of Good Hope, where the peninsula thrusts between two great currents. To the north lie the Hottentots-Holland Mountains, and beyond them the African interior.

'Come on, we can admire the view later,' Marike pressed. We followed the path south, past the cute tea-rooms and on across the mountain.

It was beautiful up there, like being on the roof of the world. As though in agreement, a raucous 'kek-kek-kek-kek' came from one side and I saw a striking bird perched on a straggly bush. Its wings and back were bluish black with white spots, and the heavy head had a pronounced crest, with a large sharp beak.

'Oh, it's a giant kingfisher,' Marike said softly. 'They don't usually come to the top of the mountain.'

'Why has he now?'

'Well, he likes to hunt from a handy perch over-

119

looking a likely pool, and dives down on fish and frogs. I bet he's making for the same place we are today.'

'And what place is that, may one enquire?'

'The reservoirs. The main two are to the right of Junction Peak over there, and there's another three smaller ones on the back table. Come on, you're not very fit for your age.'

With the admonition ringing in my ears I made an effort to keep up with her, as she strode away like a marathon walker. Only when we stopped did I tell myself it was worth the effort. Birds were everywhere, and she pointed out small laughing doves with their pink heads, Fiscal shrikes with white Vs on their backs, swifts, martins, rock thrushes, swallows. We saw two hawks whirling in the sky above us at different times; a rock kestrel and the African goshawk.

Creatures of the underbrush were everywhere too, according to Marike, but I only managed to see a small lizard, which she called a gecko, and a chameleon. Brightly coloured flowers were in abundance but I took a raincheck on knowing every last name from Marike. She made up for it though when we reached a group of rocks above the Woodhead and Hely-Hutchinson reservoirs,and settled ourselves down in the sunshine.

'The last lion was shot up here in 1802, and the elandt disappeared in 1840,' she said softly. 'The leopard went around 1870, despite many reported sightings since then. All gone now.'

I couldn't resist a nervous glance around. 'There was a lot of animals here?'

'A lot.' She looked at me. 'Once there was elephant, black rhino, Cape buffalo, elandt, hartebeeste and zebra grazing on the slopes of the mountain, and lion and leopard raided the livestock near the Castle. Hyenas scavenged around the settlement. Now, 300 years later, all of the larger mammals have been wiped out.'

'Aren't we a greedy bunch, *homo sapiens*,' I muttered.

'Not *we*, black man,' she smiled sadly. 'My lot, the whites. The black people of Africa only killed what they needed for food and clothing. It took the arrival of white men to teach them to kill for the horns and the ivory, the skins and hides, and to sell them for money. *And,* of course, to poach.'

'What's left up here now?' I managed to prevent a look over my shoulder.

'Well, there's about 50 species of mammal still up here, and the largest is the baboon, called Chacma after the Khoikhoi name for them. They live in troops of anything from 12 to 50, and don't usually attack people.'

'What do you mean, *don't usually*?' I frowned.

'People are warned not to feed them but they ignore the signs. Now the Chacma become very aggressive if you don't give them anything. There are also a few lynx, or caracal. They hunt small antelope, dassies, hares, rodents and birds, and they're not too popular with poultry owners down there. There's also the mongoose, genet, porcupine, and what's left of the smaller antelope such as grysbuck, steenbuck, duiker, and an occasional klipspringer. Oh, and some Himalayan goats that escaped from Groote Schuur Zoo.'

'You seem to know an awful lot about the place,' I said.

'I was down here to cover the visit of Sir Edmund Hillary, when he was campaigning to *Clean up Table Mountain*. Ironic isn't it? We have to have a New Zealander come and tell us we have to preserve one of the most beautiful places in the world.' I said nothing, merely staring at the beauty around us. 'I finished up doing a whole series for a magazine on the mountain itself. Do you know it's one of the richest floral areas in the world? It has double the number of species that California has, in one-third the area. The Cape Peninsula, which is an area smaller than the Isle of Wight, has over 200 more species than in the whole of England.'

'Whoa!' I held up a hand, laughing. 'How do you

remember all that stuff?'

'I wrote a lot about it, and I also have a photographic memory. Didn't I mention it? Come on, I'm starving. Let's get back for some lunch.'

The walk back was relaxed, despite my keeping an eye open for a troop of baboons or an extinct leopard or two.

Lunch itself was pleasant, accompanied by the usual bottle of chilled wine. This time it was a Boschendal Blanc de Noir, a dry wine that looked like a rosè but tasted dry and full. We ate smoked salmon and fresh green salad and talked about nothing very much until halfway through.

Suddenly we were into politics again.

Marike was staring at a Times someone had left on the next table, and she reached over and picked it up. She studied it for several seconds and when she looked up she slidd the paper across in front of me. The headline read:

NAT AMNESTY PLAN TO FREE MASS KILLERS

I tried to read on but was interrupted when she slammed a hand down on the table.

'That's the biggest piece of shit they've done yet, the bastards,' she hissed. 'Last September de Klerk was blackmailed by the ANC into releasing a large number of *political* prisoners before they'd agree to attend the negotiation summit. Among them was Robert McBride, who planted a bomb in Magoos Bar in Durban in 1986. He killed three women and injured more than 20. What the hell was political about that? Two others, Mncube and Nondula were MK terrorists trained in Mozambique, Angola and East Germany. In 1987 they laid landmines in the Messina district, killing 10 and wounding 20 others. Mncube also shot two policemen. A lot of the victims were Black. *Political?*'

'I get your point,' I said quietly. 'Now *what's* happened?'

'As if that wasn't bad enough, they now propose to include a *cover-up* clause in the constitution that will release another load of criminals onto the streets.'

'These are all Blacks?'

'No. The two sentenced to death for killing Chris Hani, Derby-Lewis and Walus, are among them. So are three AWB who gunned down seven innocent Black people in 1990. There are the Blacks who butchered the American girl, Amy Biehl, and the gunmen who murdered 11 in St James's Church here in Cape town. Look there, see the picture of the young man and his girlfriend above the headlines?'

I looked. They were a nice looking couple.

'He was a seaman from the Ukraine who just happened to go to mass that day, and he lost both legs and an arm. Is that *politics*? Michael Phama there, down the page, he's committed more murders than any one man in our country's history, and is serving 21 life sentences. But because he says he's an ANC member, he'll walk free.'

I read on. 'It applies to all criminal and civil acts committed or associated with political objectives inside and outside South Africa, up to the 1st December this year. That includes an awful lot of criminals, doesn't it?'

'Tens of thousands,' she closed her eyes. 'What a fucking mess – pardon my French. It's the White regime trying to appease the incoming Black regime. And they haven't even picked a flag or an anthem yet. Either *Nkosi Sikelel' iAfrika* or *Die Stem*.'

'Which do you think it should be?'

'No doubt in my mind. It should be *Nkosi Sikelel' iAfrika*. It was written as a hymn by a man called Enoch Sontonga, who was Tembu and a Methodist teacher, just before the turn of the century. Which is why it doesn't appeal to the Afrikaner.'

I laughed and she looked at me.

'I was just thinking what Tom told me about *Dixie*, the anthem of the Old South. Since the Civil War the

Ku-Klux-Klansmen have claimed the tune as the hymn of White supremacy. Two scholars have recently discovered it was written by a Black family called Snowden.'

She began laughing and I joined in, relieved she'd got off the previous theme. I casually flicked the paper under the table.

'Where now,' I asked, patting my stomach. 'A quiet siesta would be just the thing if I had a choice.'

'You haven't,' she pulled a face. 'We came here to see the mountain, so we're going to walk lunch off, not sleep it off. You'll thank me for it later.'

'I somehow doubt that,' I smiled. 'But lead on, McDuff.'

This time we headed north-east and came to the Eastern Table. We sat on some rocks and looked at Devil's Peak.

'The Dutch called it Windberg at first, and the English knew it as Charles' Mount,' Marike said in her travel guide voice again, but I didn't mind.

'How did it get its present name?'

'Ahh,' she grinned wisely. 'That was the same time that the tablecloth was formed. Forget all that scientific nonsense I told you the other day, this is the real truth.'

'About as true as Kennedy being killed by Oswald?'

She made a good job of ignoring me. 'Centuries ago there was a retired pirate who lived on the slopes of Windberg. His name was Van Hunks and he spent his days drinking rum and smoking his foul-smelling pipe. One day a sinister looking stranger came up to him and asked for a fill of tobacco. He congratulated the old pirate on the strength of his mixture. "I've smoked more than any man living, and I can smoke any man under the table," Van Hunks boasted. The stranger took up the challenge and offered him the kingdoms of the world against his soul.'

I was chuckling by now, and she gave me a mock glare.

124

'Soon the clouds of tobacco smoke rolled down the mountain. They smoked for days, and though the old pirate was feeling it, he was still smoking away when the stranger dropped his pipe and collapsed.'

She looked at me solemnly. 'Then Van Hunks gave him some rum and pulled his hat off.'

'And he saw the horns,' I grinned.

'And he saw the horns,' she swatted an imaginary fly from my left ear. 'So the mountain became Devil's Peak, and whenever you see the clouds driven before a really bad south-easter, then you know Van Hunks and the Devil are puffing away again.'

'Very good, but what about today?' I put an arm around her shoulders and gave her a squeeze. 'There isn't a cloud in the sky. Has he run out of tobacco?'

'In the winter months he suffers from rheumatism and can't climb the mountain, but sometimes – around now – he feels a twinge or two and stays in bed.'

'I give up,' I laughed. 'You've got an answer for everything.'

'I do have a history degree from Stellenbosch you know,' she confessed. 'It was only writing for the school newspaper that made me realise I really wanted to be a journalist.'

I climbed to my feet and helped her up. 'Well, you certainly...'

A crack rang out on the clear air, as a chip of stone from where I'd been sitting a moment ago flew off and nicked my leg. It sliced through my pants and drew blood.

'What the hell...?' I gazed down at my leg with fascination.

Only when Marike pulled me down beside her, did I realise someone had a gun out there, and we were the targets.

125

Eighteen

'Christ, someone's shooting at us,' I cried, rather unnec-cessarily.

'I know that,' she snapped. 'Where's he firing from?'

'How the hell would I know? Let's run.'

I grabbed her hand and we ran back towards the centre of the mountain. Another shot spurred us on as it pinged away behind us.

'He's behind us,' I yelled, again unneccessarily.

'Well done, hero,' she yelled back. 'Even I could tell that.'

'This is no time for sarcasm,' I retorted, and then we dropped down into lower ground.

'Keep still,' I ordered. 'I'll try to see where he's fir-ing from.'

'Listen for the *crack-thump*,' she said.

'What...?'

'The *crack-thump*. Don't you know anything about guns? There's a crack when the bullet leaves the bar-rel, and a thump when it goes past your ear, as it breaks the sound barrier...'

'This is no time for a lecture on physics, or ballis-tics, or whatever you call it,' I hissed.

'If you count the seconds between the crack and the thump you can tell how far away he is,' she finished with that smug look that women have.

'That's good,' I admitted. 'So how far away is our sniper?'

As though to help us out, two more shots came in our direction. This time, because I was listening for it, I distinctly heard the *crack-thump*.

'Well?'

'I... er... can't remember how many metres it is to the second, and I think it has something to do with the muzzle velocity as well,' she said lamely. 'Some are faster than others, but in warfare they know what weapons the enemy is using.'

'What happened to that photographic memory of yours?' It was my turn to be sarcastic, but she didn't react.

'He must be on Devil's Peak,' she muttered, shoving her head slowly over the top of the sheltered ground we lay in. 'We ran directly away from it and the shots were at our heels.'

'Too damn close to our heels for my liking,' I said angrily. She was right of course.

'It's also the only place that's higher than us.' If she was trying to make me feel useless on purpose it was definitely working.

'There hasn't been a shot for some time,' I said, striving to regain my position as the man among us. 'He must have gone.'

I don't know why I stood up then, probably the feeling that I ought to take charge of our situation in some way. I suppose I was also trying to prove what I'd just said.

Whatever the reason, I rose facing Devil's Peak and the bullet struck me from the rear. It only hit shallow on my right side, glanced off a rib and went whining harmlessly away, but it was the first time I'd ever been shot so I made the most of it.

Marike wasn't having any of it. She pulled me back down again, cursing and swearing in Afrikaans. I'll never know what she called me and I don't think I want to.

'Great,' she spat. 'There's two of them, as you've

just found out the hard way. How bad is it?'

The words were said off-handedly, and as she didn't even bother looking at me, I maintained a brave silence. The stiff upper-lip of public school when a fist lifted you up in the scrum. I was also getting mad, and action was the only recourse I'd ever pursued when that happened.

'Let's go, blondie,' I grabbed her hand and dragged her to her feet. 'My turn to come up with something this time.'

We went over the top like the poor sods in the trenches of World War I, and ran as if our lives depended on it. Which they did.

'Where are we going?' Marike cried, stumbling alongside me.

'Over here,' I yelled as bullets came at us from both directions at once, and we cleared the lip of the escarpment both screaming at the tops of our voices.

We hit rocky scrub and began tumbling and rolling in a cloud of dust. When I thought we were safely out of the line of fire, I jerked her hand to stop and had a good look around.

'That's Silverstream Ravine across our front,' Marike gasped. 'The Gorge is to our left, but it's not safe. Too much erosion.'

'Is it any safer if we go back along the top?' I asked, managing a grin in response to the scowl on her pretty face. 'No, I thought not. We'll take the gorge.'

Best not to describe that journey down. I mentioned my aversion to heights before, yet there is still a difference between standing in a cablecar, wedged between twenty-seven other people and tumbling down a mountainside with two idiots firing at you. We somehow made it onto what some optimist had marked on the map as a track, and that was where the real nightmare began.

No more shots had followed us since we'd disappeared over the lip, and I assumed we were hidden from the gunman on the Peak. We were, and by the time the second gunman had reached the lip of the gorge, we'd disappeared below the false crest further down.

Platteklip Gorge is a very steep valley with the rocks on either side standing upright like monstrous walls, and we were grateful it wasn't winter, when water would drip from them continuously to form a stream down where we were now moving. At one place Marike actually had the nerve to point to a huge smooth declining rock, and began telling me it was the *platteklip*, or flat rock after which the Gorge was named. Not surprisingly, and given the circumstances, I showed little interest at that point.

We were about two thirds of the way down when Marike suggested we stop for a few minutes rest. It was a good idea, for the more exhausted we became the more chance there was of having an accident.

We heard the sound at the same time, and looked at each other.

'So much for my idea that they'd given up,' I said quietly. 'Let's hide in that cave over there, just in case it *is* one of them.'

It wasn't really a cave, in the strict sense, but simply a dark hollow where one large boulder had come to rest across two others. I wondered irrelevantly when the next one was due to come down.

We crouched in the shadows at the back and waited to see if one of our would-be assassins was catching up, or if it was a particularly fit hiker who ran down mountains for laughs. At the speed we'd come down, I rather doubted the latter.

I was feeling around for a stone when Marike drew my attention to the stench of human excreta in our hiding place. Obviously some visitors to the mountain were not aware of the country code about burying things. Fortunately my hand closed over a handy-sized rock before I had time to change my mind.

'Shush,' she whispered, although I hadn't spoken.

Stones rattled outside and a figure went past at the run. I had time to make out that he was a Black,

129

dressed in a raincoat despite the heat, and carried a rifle at what I think they call the *low trail* in military circles.

'It's an AK47,' Marike whispered. 'Be careful.'

'What the hell do you mean, *be careful?*' I yelped quietly. 'What do you think I'm going to do?'

'You'll have to stop him,' she said firmly. 'He'll soon realise he should have caught up with us by now, then he'll either come back, or just wait and take us out as we come down.'

'Talk about *me* seeing too many movies,' I snorted in the semi-darkness. '*Take us out*, indeed. How did he manage to get up there with a bloody great rifle, anyway?'

'Why d'you think he's wearing a raincoat in the middle of summer?' she asked scathingly. 'Besides, I'm sure he could have climbed up if he'd wanted to. He looked very fit to me.'

'Great,' I muttered. 'She wants me to go out there after some athletic nut armed with an AK47. The name's O'Brien, not Bond. Can't we just call for help?'

'Phillip...'

'I'm going, I'm going.' I kissed her fiercely on the mouth and slipped quietly out of our hiding place. Our erstwhile murderer was climbing back up the crumbling path. The advantage, momentary though it was, belonged to me for he was walking with his head down, as though looking for some tell-tale sign of our whereabouts in the dust, dirt and stones.

Some instinct made him lift his head. The rifle, held now across his body with both hands, also began to lift. But he was too late, for my rock was already on its way and I was right behind it. The stone – about the size of my fist – hit him in the middle of the chest. He smashed backwards into the rock wall, stunned yet still trying to raise his rifle.

I reached him in a few bounds, intending to knock the rifle away, but he'd already figured he wasn't going to get it firing in time, and dropped it. Both fists began flailing at me and so fast were they moving that a

130

couple of roundhouses clipped me across the head. I adopted a boxing stance and began picking him off with lefts and rights, but he seemed oblivious of them.

It was then I remembered something Robbie our boxing coach at school used to say. He was an ex-sergeant major from the Army Physical Training Corps, and had been Services middleweight champion in his day.

'Never 'it a darkie in the 'ead, young gentlemen,' he'd say. 'It's made of solid rock, beggin' yer pardon Mister O'Brien. 'It 'im in the breadbasket – He'll go down like a sack of shit.'

He'd been right, of course, and I'd never been knocked out in the ring. I'd been knocked down a few times, but only with body punches, and I'd fought a few other black opponents myself where the same advice held true. Once when we'd been fighting a local club, and I was matched against a Mike Tyson lookalike, I heard old Robbie shouting, "come on the nigger – the posh one". I'd laughed so much I almost lost the match. There was no harm in old Robbie, and I often think of him.

So I sank a low right into the man's stomach and he went down on one knee, winded. I kicked away the rifle and stood over him. He began cursing in his own language, whatever that was.

'I hope you can speak English, friend,' I said angrily. 'Because unless you tell me who sent you to kill us, I'm going to do you an awful lot of damage.'

Whether or not he could speak English I never found out, for he suddenly launched himself at me, both arms wrapping around me like an octopus. He was a good six inches shorter, but seemed to have enormous arms, or at least exceptionally strong ones.

I might have been raised in the posher end of Liverpool, but I'd already proved I knew the Kirkby Kiss back in the fatherland of Potschefstroom and it was time to use it again. My arms were pinioned, but my head wasn't, and I drew it back and smacked him full in the face.

131

I heard his nose break with that sickening sound of bone and cartilage crunching and splatting at the same time. I know because it's been done to me. He released my arms and staggered back, but his foot came up into my stomach, and I folded. I knew what was coming next and straightened to avoid the knee aimed for my face. The back of my head caught him beneath the chin, and the volume of the crack as his neck broke will stay with me always.

I was looking down at the body, and ignored Marike's hand on my shoulder as she came up. I felt numb.

'It wasn't your fault,' the quiet voice came from beside me. 'It was him or us. You had to do it, Phillip.'

'You're right, of course,' I agreed. 'So why doesn't it make me feel any better?'

'I know,' she said. 'And if you didn't feel that way you wouldn't be the person I love.'

We clung together for a while and when we carried on down we left the body and the rifle where they lay. The last thing we wanted was to become involved with the police. I'd checked the man's pockets and found only a piece of paper that Marike said was an ANC membership card.

I don't remember much of the trip down, except that we cut off to the left and went along what she called the Upper Contour Path. Finally we descended a steep series of steps that brought us out to the left of the lower cableway station.

I think I said something silly about asking for a refund on our two-way tickets, and then we were in the car and Marike was driving back to the hotel.

The descent off the mountain had seemed to take hours, and when I looked at my watch I saw it had been. We'd be back in time for dinner, and then I remembered the man we'd left on the mountain.

He wouldn't be eating dinner again. Ever.

Nineteen

It took five minutes work with the hotel medical kit and several stiff whiskies to put things back in perspective.

On the way to the hotel Marike stopped at a liquor store and bought a bottle of Grouse. When we reached the hotel we went straight to my room where she called room service. A few minutes later a waiter arrived with ice and a jug of soda water.

She thrust a drink in my hands and ordered me to swallow it while she went to work on my 'minor wound' as she called it. It didn't feel minor when she doused it with old-fashioned iodine.

'The Geldenhuys cure for most things,' she said lightly, refilling my glass. 'A stiff whisky or a bonk. As you don't look up to a bonk, get that down you.'

That – and the whisky – brought a smile to my face. In no time there was another in my hand.

'Better?' she asked. I nodded and it was back to business again. 'Right, let's see what we have now. Brit journalist murdered, gay connections, involved with right-wing MP. Two attempts on our lives. What does all this tell us?'

'That the opposition is larger than we are, and far better organised.'

'It also tells us the most important thing as far as a journalist is concerned. That we're getting close to whatever we're looking for. And it's so big that the opposition are prepared to commit murder to prevent our finding it.'

'What *are* we looking for?' I asked sceptically.

'I 'even't a blerry clue, man,' she said with a heavy Afrikaner accent. 'But we do know a few things that we didn't know this morning. The man with the AK spoke in Xhosa when you hit him, and that card he had was for ANC membership. They pay R5 a month, which is big bucks when you think how many members they have. This leads to another interesting question. If Albrecht *is* behind all this, what's he doing hiring local ANC members?'

'I read somewhere they can get AK47s for R40 each,' I said reflectively. 'What's to stop a couple of local chaps making a few bob on the side?'

She gave me a sympathetic look and shook her head. 'You still don't get it, Phillip, do you? There's no way a member of the ANC would kill for an Afrikaner. Factions within the Xhosas and Zulus kill each other off all the time, and they've no compunction about killing the odd White, but they won't do his killing for him. This is a strange country to Europeans, and unless you've lived here all your life you could never understand the values placed on human life. Far more attention is paid to honour.'

'So what are you saying?' I was puzzled. 'Albrecht has nothing to do with it? The ANC killed Barnes and are after us?'

'I don't know,' she shrugged in a strangely appealing gesture of helplessness. 'I honestly don't know. We ignored the warning in the photo and now we've been targeted, like John Barnes.'

I poured another two drinks and we sat drinking for a while, absorbing our thoughts along with the Grouse, and trying to unravel whatever mystery we were involved in.

'Hang on,' I said suddenly. 'We intended to ignore the warning, but how did *they* know that? We didn't have time.'

'You're right,' she said slowly. 'We went sight-seeing, not snooping. There was no time to heed the warning.'

'Which means?'

'Oh, God...'

'Steady, that's blasphemy,' I said severely, having read up on it.

A peculiarity of South African television is that all naughty words are blanked out, but we're not just talking about four letter ones here. The use of the word 'God' is absolutely *verboten*. Sometimes the odd 'fuck' gets through, but never 'God'. Funny people. In a national poll recently, all races agreed on one thing. The greatest threat facing the country was not Communists, White racists, the ANC, APLA, or the police. It was Satan...

'We've got problems, Phillip. There must be *two* lots after us.' She tapped me on the knee suddenly. 'Hey, are you here or off somewhere in the dim recesses of your tiny mind?'

'I'm here,' I smiled. 'What if there *are* two lots of the ungodly after us? If we can find out *who* they are perhaps we can direct them against each other.'

'Not silly...' she said thoughtfully. 'I have a few ideas in mind. Tomorrow, using my press card, I'm going to delve into the archives at the newspaper library. Why don't you stay here and go through *all* of Barnes' papers? I feel there's still something we've missed in all this.'

'Sounds good to me,' I said wearily.

'How do you feel now, Phillip?' She studied me closely. 'I hate to sound corny, but I've covered a few wars around the globe and I've seen the results of killing shock.'

'I'm all right,' I assured her. 'It *was* a shock, but I'm okay now, I promise you.'

'I hope so, I really do. Because the way things are going, you might have to do it again.'

Which successfully stopped the conversation at that point, and we slowly worked our way down the bottle for the rest of the evening.

Twenty

I woke to the smell of fresh coffee being wafted under my nose and cool lips on my forehead. As I sat upright a moan of pain and anguish escaped me.

'Poor baby,' the words were cooler than the lips. 'Is it our side, or do we have we a bad head? Do we feel like a baboon has put a plank across our mouth and used it to crap from?'

'Such crudeness ill becomes a lady,' I croaked. 'Particularly at this time of the night.'

'Hah,' she said loudly. 'For your information, hero, it's nine o'clock in the morning, which makes it almost afternoon for most of us. I'm off to the Argus library. You'll find the number by your telephone, should you happen to get something done before I come back. Ciao.'

Once more cool lips brushed the skin above my eyebrows and the door closed behind her with a loud slam that I thought was childish.

Two cups of coffee later and I found the strength to dive under a cold shower. After I dressed I tipped the results of John Barnes' stay in the Republic onto the bed. I didn't trust my shaking hands to negotiate my face with a razor.

By eleven I couldn't stand it any longer and traipsed downstairs to see our little friend Charlie

behind the bar. I marvelled at the disparity in appearance between him and the other Charlie of my acquaintance. They both had one thing in common, however.
Both had fantastic hang-over cures, and little Charlie
made one up for me with a little knowing grin.

By the time I got back to the room I was feeling
much better, and an hour later I was ordering sand-
wiches and chicken legs from room service. I thought
about a beer, but only for a moment, and settled for
more coffee.

By three o'clock I'd found it, and waited impatient-
ly for the return of the lovely Marike so I could gloat.

§

I was on the bed dozing peacefully among the debris of
paper when the door crashed open with a noise that
shot me what seemed like six feet in the air.

'Why on earth can't you leave and enter a room
like normal people? Quietly.' I complained.

'Because at this time of the day normal people
wouldn't still be lying on their backs,' she grinned
cheerfully.

'I bet you haven't had a single twinge in your head
all day,' I groaned.

'No. I felt great. Even better when I found out
what all this was about.'

'I've had some degree of success myself,' I sniffed.
'Which is why I allowed Morpheus to get a grip on me.'

'Good. Tell me about it while I organise a drink.
Did we finish the bottle last night?'

'You know damn well we did,' I groaned again. 'So
you're some kind of female sponge, there's no need to
boast about it.'

Marike ordered herself a whisky and soda. When
she raised an enquiring eyebrow to me I shuddered and
shook my head. She laughed and replaced the receiver.

'Okay, smarty-pants, what've you got?'

I dipped into the pile and extracted a few pages of

A4, neatly typewritten and stapled together. I tossed it across.

'Read it if you like, but the basic point is the involvement of the US in the internal politics of South Africa. It has to do with their wooing of the new government after the April elections, and how much control they can expect to have *within* that government.'

'Interfering in the internal politics of another country is contrary to the rulings of the United Nations,' she said pedantically, as though quoting something she'd read.

'Right,' I snorted. 'So what have they been doing since the Second World War? Even Vietnam was an invasion of that policy, though I don't knock the principles behind it. You should know a lot more about it than me, anyway.'

'I do,' she looked smug. 'I've been going down the same path. Listen to this. "Up until the mid-80s, the FBI and the National Security Agency kept the SA embassy under the kind of surveillance reserved for hostile powers like the former Soviet Union. Armscor's efforts to develop weapons of mass destruction – and to acquire the necessary US technology – were part of the reason. Another was Pretoria's own espionage".'

'What's *Armscor*, and what does that last sentence mean?'

A light knock signalled the arrival of her drink, and she didn't reply until she took a long sip and sat down.

'*Armscor* is a private company that makes weapons. All kinds from pistols to rockets. Government involvement has been rumoured, but never proven. Also, America feared that President Botha's SA agents were targeting ANC officials in the US for wet work.'

'Wet...what?'

'Wet work. It's espionage agency slang for assassinations. In 1988 a member of the ANC, Dulcie September, was murdered in Paris. The US and other Western governments believed Pretoria had mounted a campaign to assassinate ANC officials on their territory, and Washington came close to declaring SA a *Terrorist State*.'

'What about the ANC detention camps that I've read about?' I said. 'There's a report here that 10 South Africans are being held at a camp in Tanzania, and they've been tortured and ill-treated. They also have camps in Angola, Mozambique, Transkei, and God knows where else.'

'Hundreds of people have disappeared the same way,' she shrugged. 'The Motsuenyane report revealed that 70 ANC members in exile had been executed, beaten to death, committed suicide, or died of *natural causes* in ANC camps. Amnesty International have a list of another 200 missing after being seen entering their camps.'

'The difference is, the ANC terrorists were *freedom fighters* to the rest of the world and could do what they liked, while the SA government was condemned no matter what.'

'Okay, they're nasties who sound as bad as each other, but horrible as it is, where does it get us? From what you say, this has all been published before, and presumably it will be forgotten under the new negotiations, so what angle was Barnes after? I thought I had something there for a minute.'

'I think you *do* have something, Phillip. According to the newspapers there's a headlong rush by the business community to appoint ANC-linked individuals to senior positions. I know it sounds sick but it's survival, I suppose. SA Breweries have made an ANC executive, Saki Macozoma, business development manager, and a former Robben Island prisoner, Soto Nudukwana, is corporate affairs manager.'

'Yes, but what...?'

'Armscor have just appointed Yacoob Abba Omar as public-relations manager. Omar is a former member of MK. He'll now serve on the management board which, and I quote: "gives him access to the very heart of decision-making in the giant corporation". One day a terrorist – raiding across the border into South Africa – the next in a controlling position with one of the biggest arms makers in Africa. One with nuclear capabilities. Makes you think, doesn't it?'

'Are you trying to say they've got a nuclear bomb here?' I stared at her.

'Not one. Six. The Times published an article about the Y-plant at Valindaba, where uranium is upgraded. The enriched uranium was used to make six nuclear devices, and US officials have been sniffing around the Times and the plant.'

'Christ,' I breathed.

'Oh, it's not top secret news,' she said. 'In 1991, George Bush imposed additional sanctions on Armscor because of its missile programme. This was followed by the indictment of Armscor and subsidiaries, Kentron and Fuchs, on hi-tech arms smuggling charges. Now to the nitty-gitty, and you can be very proud of me for this, because I know I am,' she said modestly.

'Get on with it, woman,' I growled in mock anger. 'I hope you don't write like you talk; newspapers would be thick as novels.'

She threw a cushion at me. 'I have a friend in government circles who owes me a favour and I gave him a ring. A commission is being set up to look into Armscor's activities, and he read me a list of members. The chairman of the commission is none other than our friend Kobus Albrecht. I'm having another drink. Want one?'

This time I nodded dumbly, and she rang for service.

'Something else I picked up at the archives,' she continued. 'Since July, Frelimo guerrillas from Mozambique have been arrested for training township self-defence units on the East Rand and in Natal, and for supplying firearms to the IFP. Reports from Mozambique say the tide is about to turn in the government's favour, and large arms shipments are said to be

140

coming from the south.'

'Are you saying the ANC, through Armscor, are going to sell the Mozambican government more firepower because *their* opposition – Frelimo – are being nice to the Zulus?'

'Why not? They already have training camps up there. With Albrecht on the commission, he can sweep it under the carpet.'

'But why would he want to help the A...? Of course, the blackmail thing!'

'Bit slow today, aren't we? That's right, the *blackmail thing*. Which makes our next move obvious, don't you think?'

'Obvious. Of course.' A knock came to the door, heralding room service. I felt in need of a drink now and stood up to get it. 'What *is* our obvious next move, you infuriating female?'

'Simple,' she beamed at me. 'We just have to get into Albrecht's castle and find some proof. How about tonight?'

Twenty-One

We dined in the hotel that evening, not wishing to push our luck by wandering around town where we could be easily spotted by the invisible enemy out there. They had the advantage of knowing what *we* looked like but we didn't know them. And if Marike was right, there was not one enemy but two. We hadn't discussed the second lot, because if they did indeed exist, then neither of us wanted to face it.

Marike was on a roll, and all for going in that night, but I would have none of it. For one thing I was still feeling a little delicate from the excesses of the previous night, and a throbbing ache in my bruised ribs. For another we needed equipment and some sort of plan.

Marike feigned disgust at my caution, 'Ag man, *'n Boer maak 'n plan.*'

I pulled a face over my brandy glass.

'Its an old Afrikaner expression,' she poked a dainty tongue at me. It brought back memories of our nights together. 'It means *a farmer will make and plan.* In other words, O doubting one, *we'll come up with something in time.*'

'Not good enough,' I shook my head. 'You saw the walls, the gates, the guards.... What do you think the inside will be like? I noticed surveillance cameras all around the place for starters. I agree he probably *has* got something to hide in there, but that's all the more reason to be prepared.'

'I suppose you're right,' she conceded, much to my surprise. 'Tomorrow night then. We'll go shopping in the morning.'

'I'll drink to that,' I drained my glass and ordered two more. 'I'm beginning to like the white man's firewater.'

'And what about their women?' she asked coyly, using the cover of the long tablecloth to do rude things to my thigh with a bare foot.

§

We overslept, then over-indulged in a session of morning delight, with the result that breakfast was almost over when we got down. Again I sensed, rather than actually saw, censorship in the faces of the few remaining guests in the dining room.

When I pointed it out to Marike she merely smiled and placed an obvious hand over mine.

'It will take a long time for the people in this country to lose a lot of their prejudices – if they ever do. Certainly not the older generations. My family would have a fit if they saw us here like this, knowing we shared the same bed. Strangely enough, if my father was still alive, he would have accepted you more easily than any of them. He always respected education, no matter who had it.'

'We'd find prejudice in the UK,' I said quietly. 'I've told you about my parents. My sister's different, you'll get on well together, and my mother's people are from the Carribean and care only for what's inside a person. They have an expression, *a man is a man*, which just about sums it up. My mother was the one who *got up herself*, as they say in Liverpool, when she married a doctor.'

'I'm looking forward to meeting them all,' she said, and there was no sarcasm in her voice.

143

We'd never discussed the future, both being of an age and present disposition that living for the day was enough, but now deeper thoughts were beginning to break the surface of our mutual and unspoken acceptance of the present.

By tacit consent we dropped the subject and began to draw up a list of our requirements for breaking into a person's house. We discussed movies, books, factual police cases that Marike had dealt with; in fact all the precedents we could come up with. We finished with a list as long as your arm with enough gear to outfit a small mercenary force.

'Whoa,' I said in the end. 'We're looking at it all wrong. Neither of us has the training for this kind of thing.'

'All right, what's the alternative?'

'Simple, as you keep saying. We walk up to the front gate and ask to be let in.'

She gave me a long, penetrating, and thoroughly disconcerting, look. I was ready for the explosion, but it never came.

'Why not?' she said. 'We could take turns going to the bathroom and looking around. Say we had bad bladders or something.'

'You think it's silly,' I sulked.

'No, you're right. It makes more sense than scaling the walls, laying out the guards, killing any Rottweilers they have in the grounds, knocking out the cameras, and breaking into the house. Only I'll be the one with the bad bladder.'

I started to protest but she reached across and placed a finger on my lips.

'I've got a marvellous little camera for situations like this and I wouldn't trust it to a great oke like you. Now let's get out of here, I think they want to get ready for lunch.'

§

We spent a pleasant day browsing around Cape Town. I

could have spent a week poring through the old book-shops in Long Street alone, but Marike dragged me away. We lunched at the Cape Sun Hotel, then strolled around the Castle, which was in the shape of a five-pointed star, with stone walls more than 10 metres high, now the headquarters of the Western Cape Military Command.

We visited the South African Museum where there was an exhibit of the Great Trek, and I gazed in awe at a wagon from that time. The written details could not do justice to its sheer size and solidity. 18 foot long and 5 foot wide, it was heavy and immensely strong, built of assegai wood, wild pear, blackwood, stinkwood, and ironwood. They're hard to find today. They were all iron-hard, except for the bed which was made of planks of yellowwood. The front wheels were much lower than the back, and were seven inches across to make the going easier in sand or mud.

'Over 150 years ago my ancestors travelled a 1000 miles north in one of these,' Marike's voice spoke softly in my ear.

'Why?' I asked.

'For freedom, and to escape the English and their tax collectors. A home on wheels, a ship to sail the hostile *veldt* and the vast interior.'

'You read that somewhere,' I accused with a smile.

'I did,' she admitted. 'An old South African writer.'

'You Afrikaners have a wonderful heritage to be proud of,' I said as we left the museum, and she turned her head quickly to see if I was being sarcastic. I wasn't. 'It's a pity the damage your Dr Verwoerd caused to your people, as well as the other races.'

'Yes,' was all she said.

She then took me to the National Gallery and the Malay Museum, and was about to drag me into the Jewish Museum when I held a hand up.

'Enough,' I pleaded. 'No more museums or picture galleries, please. It's nothing personal, some of my best friends are Jews, but let's get a drink instead.'

She laughed at the old joke and gave in.

145

We arrived in Hout Bay early and strolled along the beach. A bronze leopard looked down on us from a rock below the cliff road. My walking encyclopaedia said it was done by a local sculptor, and was 1.4 metres high, weighing 295 kilos. We had dinner in a seafood restaurant on the wharf. The linefish of the day was *kabeljou*, served with an excellent Hollandaise sauce, new potatoes and gem squash.

Marike asked if I fished and I shook my head.

'I'm afraid if you ate anything caught in the River Mersey you'd turn green and glow in the dark. British waters are terribly polluted now, and a lot of the fish brought in are found to have high levels of mercury in them.'

She shook her head sympathetically.

'My father was a keen fisherman. Every chance he had he'd be off fly fishing, or down to the coast with friends. He had a plaque over his desk with the Fisherman's Prayer on, and it made us all laugh because it was so applicable'

> '...*Lord, grant this day I catch a fish,*
> *So large that even I,*
> *In telling of it afterwards,*
> *Shall have no need to lie...*'

'That's it,' she said delightedly. 'How do you know it if you aren't a fisherman?'

'I know a poem about the moon,' I laughed. 'But I've never been there.'

The meal had passed pleasantly, and at eight-thirty we were pulling up outside the massive gates of Albrecht's modern mansion. It was the same security guard and he must have recognised us for he was on the phone right away. A minute later the gates began to move aside noiselessly.

Van Rensberg was waiting next to the Mercedes. With a curt nod by way of greeting he led the way to the lift. No words were exchanged and this time we stopped on the fourth floor.

From the lift we stepped straight into a magnificent lounge. Taking up almost the entire floor of the house, it was filled with artefacts – the most incredible mixture of antique and modern. There were Queen Anne chairs, a Regency escritoire, a Georgian desk. Occupying equal prominence were coffee tables of steel and glass, deep couches and easy chairs of modern design, and black lacquer display units with books, records and CDs.

The walls were light pink, and the floor grey tiles with pink scatter rugs of Chinese design. It should have been awful but somehow it all fitted. It showed that the owner was both wealthy and progressive.

The wealthy and progressive owner was sitting rather primly in one of the Queen Anne's, and made no attempt to get up when we entered.

'Mr O'Brien and Miss Geldenhuys again,' he said archly. 'To what do we owe the honour this time? Have you found the killer of that poor boy yet?'

'We have a pretty good idea,' I sat down without being asked, and Marike followed suit. 'We'll have a couple of whiskies and soda if you're pouring, thank you, Gerrit.'

The short man frowned but did not look at Albrecht for permission. Instead he moved across to a tray of drinks on a side table and began pouring.

'So, you have someone in mind, Mr O'Brien?' Albrecht said.

'Yesterday two men tried to kill us on Table Mountain. On the way to the airport a man in a car tried to shoot us. Because of these attempts on our lives we felt the need for precautions.'

'Precautions?' Van Rensberg handed us the drinks with bad grace.

'When we go out now, we always leave our destination with the hotel owner,' Marike smiled sweetly at him. 'Then if we're not back around the time we say, he will get in touch with the police.'

'As for your initial question, Mr Albrecht,' I said

politely. 'Let me tell you a story. Once there was a right-wing politician who had to lean to the left over certain things. This was because he was bent – sexually that is – and the people on the left found out and threatened to tell his people on the right. It was a kind of double jeopardy because the friend our politician was poking happened to be Black. Not only was he Black, he was also a journalist, and he found out about a certain commission the politician was going to head. By the way, where's the nice young chap who served us last time?'

I paused as Albrecht shifted uncomfortably in his seat. I looked over at van Rensberg and his face was impassive. Receiving no answer I carried on with my game.

'This commission was quite important, as far as things that go bang were concerned, and when he found that the journalist was interested in more than sex, our politician thought he would kill all the birds at the same time; the blackmail bird, the gay bird, and the snoopy bird. This way all his problems would be over.'

I turned to Marike and grinned. 'How am I doing so far?'

'Very good,' she smiled. 'I bet the boys are impressed.'

'We're not,' van Rensberg snapped. 'In fact if you don't get out of here immediately I shall call the police myself. I don't know what you are trying to achieve, either of you, but Mr Albrecht will not be intimidated by you or anyone else. Now get out.'

I suddenly had a foolish feeling. If we were right, what was the point in their calling our bluff,? Only then did it occur to me that perhaps we were wrong.

I downed my drink in one while I tried to think, but even that small courtesy was denied me.

'Now!' van Rensberg ordered and glared at someone over our heads.

I touched Marike and we stood up. Behind us was the collection of muscles from the club. He stood by the lift and had a plaster strip over his nose.

There wasn't much to say really, so we didn't bother. Albrecht said nothing either, merely sat there with a slightly sick expression.

'If you've got any nasty ideas, boys, don't forget our precautions,' Marike reminded them.

'How could we?' van Rensberg actually tried to smile. The effect was hideous, not unlike the eunuch of last night. Perhaps they went for the same facials. 'You're talking nonsense, so why should we bother with you? I've checked up on you, Miss Geldenhuys, and I would suggest that you go back to reporting major wars, and leave politics to those who understand them.'

A long speech for the little man and I was almost convinced he was genuine. Almost.

The pocket Schwarzenegger was holding the lift open for us and Marike stepped in. As I went to follow he suddenly sank a vicious punch into my stomach. I went down on one knee, gasping for air and felt a hand lift my head up.

'That's enough, Willie,' van Rensberg barked, and my chin dropped down on my chest. A foot in the back propelled me forward into the lift and my assailant followed and pressed the button.

'Touch him again and I will kill you, *dwerkie*' I heard Marike hiss, but being called a dwarf didn't seem to bother him and he gave a contemptuous laugh. He was probably used to it.

On the ground floor he supported me easily with one hand and threw me into the back of the car.

'I still owe you, you black bastard,' he growled.

'Not if I see you first, Willie,' I managed to get out, before we were off in a crash of gears towards the gate.

About about half a mile away Marike stopped the car under a street light and turned round to check on me.

'I'll be okay,' I managed to sit up. 'It just took the wind out of me, that's all. I should have expected it.'

'Looks like we blew it,' she pulled a face. 'Were we that wrong about everything?'

'I'm not so sure,' I muttered. 'Let's get back to the hotel and have another look at the papers. There must be something else.'

§

Some time later, fingers wrapped around a stiff Scotch, and my stomach muscles feeling a lot better following a gentle massage from Marike, I was sitting on my bed poring through Barnes' papers for the umpteenth time. His notes for the forthcoming article on arms to Mozambique were similar to those we'd put together, and Albrecht's involvement with the commission was not exactly a major secret. There was certainly nothing among them that would indicate a motive for murder.

I smiled as I heard a thump next door. Marike had gone to her own room to take a shower and was letting me know she'd be joining me soon.

I decided to forsake *poring* for a session of *pawing*, congratulated myself on the wordplay, and cleared everything off the bed in anticipation. I took a quick shower, and was mildly surprised that Marike wasn't already in bed when I'd finished. I threw on a dressing-gown and knocked on the wall to hurry her up, then turning a bedside lamp on I lay down to wait.

The ringing of the telephone woke me. I glanced at my watch and was surprised to see it was nearly midnight. I'd been asleep for nearly two hours. The bed beside me was still empty.

'Sorry to disturb you at this hour, Mr O'Brien,' I recognised the voice of the night receptionist. 'But we have an outside call for you.'

I grunted something and Marike's voice came on the line.

'Phillip. Don't say anything, darling, please. Just do what they say. They...'

There was a pause before a familiar voice came on.

'Collect everything you have on the business we

150

discussed earlier, including all John Barnes' papers. Bring them to the house at 9 o'clock in the morning, and if we are satisfied the woman will be released. You will not leave a message with anyone. If you do, we will know. If you disobey these instructions in any way, or try to pull something, you will never see her again.'

'One thing,' I said quickly. 'I agree but make it the Waterfront, the open-air theatre, 8 o'clock. If you harm her...'

'You'll do what?' van Rensberg sneered. 'You're hardly in a position to make threats, O'Brien. If you...'

'The Waterfront, 8 o'clock,' I snapped, and slammed the phone down. It was a hard thing to do, but going to the house would have been madness and van Rensberg knew it. We'd have been history before they'd served pre-lunch drinks.

I went next door and found everything as it should be. Except that Marike wasn't there. A damp towel was on the floor of the bathroom, and her dressing-gown was tossed on the bed. The wardrobe door stood open and I assumed they'd allowed her to get dressed.

It didn't take a detective to discover how they got in. The window at the end of the corridor led onto a fire escape, and it was open. I returned to the room and made some coffee.

I drank without tasting, and began cursing and blaming everything and everyone. Marike for not locking her door; the hotel for slack security; van Rensberg for taking her... but myself most of all. I should have guessed they'd pull some stunt like this. We hadn't been wrong, but we'd been bluffed long enough to get back to the hotel and cancel any message we might have left. Not that we'd left any in the first place, but they didn't know for sure. It had worked. Only too well as it turned out.

I should have seen it, and I spent the rest of the night berating myself. Except for the few hours that I dozed fitfully.

Twenty-Two

Cape Town's Victoria and Alfred Waterfront is one of the finest waterfront developments in the world. Every day it is added to and developed even more.

Most of the old dock workings have been given a facelift and a new lease of life. The main group of old railway sheds have been renovated into one massive shopping and cinema complex, with a central walk-through on two floors. Around this are other buildings, customs houses, shipping offices, cargo deposits; all adapted and added to for commercial use.

Cafes and restaurants are everywhere, from an authentic American soda-bar to a jazz bar that specialised in Creole food. Again I was reminded of my initial impression of the American influence on so many things here, and Marike's agreement that it was going to get worse as the US came back into the market-place of South Africa. Or better, depending on your taste and point of view.

The thousands of visitors who pass the jetty on Quay 5 each day are unaware of its significance in the present history of South Africa. It was from here that hundreds of people who fought in the struggle against apartheid were taken across to Robben Island.

Both would one day become national monuments in an ANC world, Marike had predicted, during the two hours we had managed to fit in down here, earlier in the week. Within ten years the present reminders of the men who had opened up this country would be gone. Within fifty there would be little to show that Whites had been here for 400 years.

Maybe it was a good thing, I'd murmured.

Statues of Mandela and his freedom fighters would replace them, she had added, and the man who had made it all possible, F.W. de Klerk, would be remembered as just another White oppressor. Again I'd been reminded that blood was thicker than water, and while I agreed she had a point or two, I still maintained that after centuries of being treated as no more than farm animals, who could blame the ANC?

But that morning I was there to appreciate neither the architecture nor the history of the place. As I'd hoped, it wasn't crowded at that time, but still had its fair share of early morning visitors.

The theatre was a small amphitheatre that consisted of wooden slats fixed to concrete steps going away from the semicircular stage. The back was a solid block wall.

The only performance going on at that early hour was the real-life drama in which I played a major part.

I was looking down on the open-air theatre from a vantage point on the second floor balcony that traversed the front of the huge building. I was on the left, seated outside the Sportsman's Cafe and drinking black coffee. I couldn't face food.

I'd been there for an hour, and during that time had counted three people I could be sure had taken up vantage points, but as this was not my field of expertise there could have been more.

On the other side of the theatre was the Ferryman's Pub, with its open area of tables and benches. Seated at one with a newspaper was a Black. He was as surreptitious as dandruff on Ronald Reagan's Grecian 2000, for he spent more time looking at the theatre than at the words in front of him. Standing

153

against the wall that ran from the theatre in my direction was another Black, who was gazing at the boats in the basin with intense interest. He had been there when had I first arrived – so how long does it take to look at a few boats? He also spent a lot of time looking towards the theatre on his right. The third man was the most obvious, because I knew him – my little pal with plaster on his nose, and he'd been seated in front of the stage for the last fifteen minutes.

It was now ten minutes to eight. Next to my chair was John Barnes' briefcase, filled with all the papers as requested. I drank my coffee slowly. I had no plan, and I needed none. In ten minutes I would walk down there and hand over the briefcase. In return I would get Marike back, and that was all that mattered to me. They'd won, but I didn't give a tupenny toss. It was over.

At one minute to eight I rose and picked up the briefcase. I walked down the wide staircase, with its nautical design that matched the balcony and everything else around, and stood by the mast in the open square above the theatre.

There was no sign of Marike and I went no further. The boat watcher was about ten yards away, but he made no pretence of watching anything but me now, and stood with his back to the wall. The man outside the pub had laid down his newspaper, and the muscular Willie gazed at the backdrop of the stage.

I heard my name called and looked up. Marike stood at the balcony railing, flanked by two white men that I hadn't seen before.

'Give the briefcase to Willie,' I heard van Rensberg's voice behind me. 'Try anything and your lady friend will get hurt.'

I turned and gazed at the smaller man with loathing. 'Where's Albrecht? Or does he just let you do his dirty work without supervision?'

He laughed with genuine amusement. 'You've got it wrong. *He* does *my* dirty work. He likes to pretend it's

154

the other way around.'

'I did get it wrong,' I admitted. 'I thought you were the power behind the throne, and you turn out to *be* the throne.'

'I looked up again and Marike managed a weak smile. Although dressed in jeans and a sweater she looked almost regal next to van Rensberg's two louts.

I turned and moved slowly down the steps, handing the briefcase to the seated Willie, and half turning away, and my eyes taking in several things at once. The man by the pub was slumped over the table as though sleeping off the night before. A cry made my eyes flick up to Marike and there was something different about her now. She was alone.

I heard the voice of the man in front of me, '...not going anywhere... both going to be fuckin' dead, you cocky black son...'

He was halfway to his feet when I hit him, and this time I didn't get his nose by accident. I aimed for the white plaster in the middle of his face. He hadn't been expecting it and the force knocked him backwards, catching his legs in the seats and he fell down hard on his back. Both hands flew up to the damaged area and I saw the gun poking out of the waistband of his trousers.

Another cry from Marike suddenly made me think of van Rensberg, but the blow on the side of my head told me I was too late. I went down in a heap and through a haze saw him reach across for the briefcase. I grabbed hold of his ankle but his other leg drove into my injured side and I let go.

I was still struggling to get up when I heard Marike's voice in my ear and she was helping me. People were beginning to gather, as people gather all over the world when some nasty event happens, and I knew it wouldn't be long before the police arrived.

'Which..way?' I groaned.

'He went that way, towards the lifeboat station, but you're in no condition to...'

'I'm going to get the little bastard,' I growled, and lurched off in the direction he'd taken.

I went past the glassed-in lifeboat, unable to admire the clean lines of the red vessel, and across towards the Victoria and Alfred Hotel. A gardener was pouring water into the thirsty plants outside and I paused to grab the hose and spray my face and neck. He thought this was a great joke and was laughing uproariously when I thrust it back into his hands.

I went up the steps three at a time and into the hotel lobby. Van Rensberg was just disappearing through the arch at the far end and I gave chase. Outside was a line of tables at which a few diners were having breakfast. He went left and I followed along the harbour's edge and around another corner, just in time to see him go down among a pile of tables and chairs outside a cafe. He was up and away before I could reach him but I was closing the gap.

He darted left again into a tall brick building encased in scaffolding. Inside, a rickety staircase ran up to the next floor. It was an old grain warehouse, and a gantry reached out of double doors above the wharf below. It even had the chains attached.

I stood still for a few moments, breathing heavily. I told myself that something had to be done about my fitness level. It wasn't as though I could blame it on smoking, because I didn't. I listened carefully but there was no noise inside the building.

I then did an incredibly stupid thing.

I walked over to the loading door with the gantry and looked out. In my defence I suppose it was to see if van Rensberg had managed to sneak past me. Maybe he'd been below all the time, and was now legging it along the jetty.

I knew he wasn't when the shoulder hit me in the back and I shot forward out of the door.

It was twenty feet to the concrete wharf below, hardened over many decades. There was a wide selection of bollards at the edge.

What saved me was van Rensberg's enthusiasm. If he'd just knocked me out of the doorway I'd have trickled over the lip and made a sickening mess below. Instead he thrust me out with wild abandon towards the gantry.

I stretched out, prayed, and closed my eyes, though in what order I don't remember. My hands grabbed and the links stopped them sliding down, but the shock of my falling body nearly tore my arms from their sockets. I wrapped my legs around the chain and hung on.

When my body stopped swinging I began to go down hand over hand, keeping my legs around the chain for support. I vaguely saw the cause of my predicament running off along the wharf, but there was nothing I could do about it. The chain ran out about six feet above the concrete.

The family Blob were strolling past, all slurping ice-creams and it wasn't 9 o'clock yet. The mother screamed as I landed at her feet, and I mumbled an apology.

For a moment it looked like Dad was going to have words with the uppity Black who had dropped from the sky and put the shits up his lady, but the expression on my face decided him otherwise.

It was a mixture of fear and anger. Anger took precedence and I took off in the direction I'd last seen Albrecht's PA going in. I rounded the corner in time to see him clamber over the rails of a yacht. I didn't have enough energy to clamber anywhere, and I jumped down from the wharf, landing heavily on the deck, and looked up into the barrel of a gun. I don't know the difference, but it looked to be a pretty large calibre from my angle .

'You don't learn, do you?' van Rensberg was screaming at me from several feet away. 'Your sort never do. Only the hard way.'

'You were going to kill us,' I panted. 'What did you expect...?'

'Expect? I expect nothing from you, you black...' the bullet hit me in the shoulder and I fell back against the cabin hatch. I couldn't believe he'd actually shot me until the pain started.

'Stop! That's enough,' a familiar voice came from behind me. I moved my head with difficulty and saw Tom Jackson, pointing a similar gun at Van Rensberg.

Tom was back, I thought, as the first waves of shock began to numb me. Everything would be all right now, *Tom was back*. His next words poured over me like a douse of cold water.

'What the fuck have you been playing at, you fool,' he climbed over the rails, and I thought he was addressing me. 'Why try and kill these people? You know the girl's a journalist, don't you?'

'Of course I know,' the little man spat, but the gun didn't waver from its target. 'If you'd *been* here you'd know about them finding out practically everything. What choice was there?'

'Choice?' the big man said softly. 'There's always a choice. You made the wrong one when you killed Barnes, you asshole. I've just found out you fools were behind it. *Someone's* bound to check up when a news-man gets killed.'

'Why...?' I asked weakly.

'It's what I do, Phil,' Tom said sadly. 'Mr Fix It. Interfering in the business of other countries. I suppose you know about the arms deal? Well, the US government is backing it because they see an alliance between Mozambique and South Africa being the first step to consolidating Black Africa. The new government here will be making the same kind of play on the rest of its border neighbours, Angola and Zambia. Then Malawi, Uganda, Zaire...'

'Why...?' I croaked again. The pain made my mouth dry.

'Why! Why do we do anything? *Stability*, would be the politicians answer, I suppose, but pragmatists might say it was so the good old US of A could control investment on the African continent.'

'He must be killed,' van Rensberg wasn't giving up, and was beginning to sound like a long-playing record. 'The girl too, they know too much now.'

'Oh, I'm sure we can get them to promise to keep their mouths shut. Isn't that right, Phil?'

'No, it isn't right!' Marike's voice came from somewhere behind us. 'A man has been killed; two if you count the one we had to kill in self-defence. And despite what Albrecht is, the poor man has been blackmailed into all this.'

She came and knelt beside me.

Van Rensberg began giggling and I heard the hatch behind us slide open.

Twenty-Three

'Thank you, Miss Guldenhuys, for that sympathetic allusion to my innocence, but I'm afraid you're wasting your time.' Kobus Albrecht came out onto the deck. 'Where are the crew, Gerrit? I think we need to get away from here'

'Ask the American,' van Rensberg snapped. 'I think he took them out while we were concentrating on this one.' His gun was still pointing at me so he needed no other reference.

'That's a nuisance,' Albrecht muttered. 'We'll have to run it around to Hout Bay ourselves.'

'I don't understand...' Marike said. I hoped she was playing for time. I hoped she had a plan. I hoped for anything other than what was going to happen. '...If you were not being blackmailed, then why kill John Barnes?'

'I was not being blackmailed. Not about being homosexual – and not concerning my fondness for black men. I *was*, however, being used. John was using our... relationship to find out lots of things he shouldn't have.'

'Like changing sides...' I muttered.

'Oh, no. I've never changed sides. I've only ever worked for one master since my early days in parliament.'

'The ANC...' Marike said in surprise.

'Good heavens, no. Both Gerrit and I work for the Americans, Miss Geldenhuys, always have done. When they told me to join the ANC, I did. It was no skin off my nose, as they say. We're all heading for a united South Africa, after all.'

'Let's get it right,' Tom said loudly. 'You're both in it for the money, and when America gets a say in the running of the country, I'm sure you'll clean up with forecasted shares and insider trading. So don't try talking ideals about peace or any of that shit.'

'I wouldn't dream of it,' Albrecht shrugged. 'But don't forget the little bit of power I also crave. Nelson's already said he needs White experience and they're welcome to mine. Now, there are members of the public over there who are trying to decide whether the guns you two are pointing are for real, or whether we're in the process of making a movie. Perhaps you can escort these two down below, Mr Jackson, while Gerrit and I take us out.'

Tom hesitated, which was what van Rensberg was waiting for. I saw the muzzle of his gun begin to traverse away from me.

'Tom!' I yelled.

He dropped to one knee and fired before I finished the warning. The little man pulled the trigger at the same time and I saw his gun slide across the deck as he slammed onto it and lay still.

Albrecht was no slouch for his age and was already diving across the deck after the gun before van Rensberg was down. He raised it and turned in triumph. Only to have Marike's foot strike his wrist and send the weapon away on its journeys again.

He made a grab for her legs but she executed a spin and he collected a foot alongside his right ear with enough force to make him go very limp. Across the deck van Rensberg lay very still, and Marike crossed over to him and placed a professional finger on his throat.

161

She looked at me and shook her head. She moved over to Tom and it was only then that I noticed he'd been shot. He'd dragged himself into a sitting position against a stanchion, and was breathing heavily through the mouth.

'He's been shot through the chest,' she called. 'It doesn't look good, Phillip.'

'I should have stayed in basketball, Phil,' he mumbled.

'Get an ambulance,' I said weakly. The pain in my shoulder was bad, but I could move it to the side so nothing vital was damaged.

'It's too late now. The police will have to be informed.' I heard Marike her calling orders to the crowd in English and Afrikaans, and I must have drifted away.

§

I woke up in hospital and felt a cool hand on my forehead.

'It's over,' she said. 'Albrecht's in jail and despite the political situation, extensive enquiries are being made. But they won't get anywhere. The ANC are too powerful now.'

'How's Tom?' I asked.

'Tom Jackson is dead.'

'Damn. We'd be dead too if it wasn't for him. Was he CIA?'

'Probably,' Marike was close to tears. 'What a mess... they'll find someone else to do their dirty work.'

'Who, the ANC – or the Americans?'

'Both,' she spat, and I had no answer for that.

Twenty-Four

We left Cape Town, and Southern Africa, on a day that was filled with sunshine and hope. There were no clouds, and no Cape Doctor blowing us inside out.

The mountain looked fantastic as we flew past, and I almost forgot I'd nearly been killed on it. It is a strange place, Africa – a land of contrasts, certainly. One day perhaps it will all come right, and the different races can live together as equals. But it will take a long time.

On this dark, brooding continent – torn apart by the warfare of many centuries – somewhere my people had their origins. I was one of the lucky ones; a black man with an education, and for possibly the first time in my life I was grateful for it.

I squeezed the hand of the woman by my side, and wondered if our children might one day make a difference, but somehow I doubted it.

I also thought of the words of Cassius Clay – in Zaire for his defence of the World Championship. When an interviewer asked him what he thought of Africa, Cassius smiled and said, 'I'm just real glad my folks took the boat trip when they did.'

I suppose that's the way I felt about it myself. Of course, I would like to come back again one day, when things have settled down.

But again, that's what people say who enjoy the luxury of a passport to the other side of the globe.

§

ONE YEAR LATER

I sat in Neville Ndongo's office sipping a glass of single malt, listening to him heap eloquent praise upon my humble shoulders.

My book on the build-up to the elections in South Africa had been the first in the bookshops, and on the non-fiction best seller list for nearly eleven months. Neville had outdone himself – editing, publishing, advertising and distributing it within three weeks of the election itself.

There was much in it that did not meet with his approval, but in this I had been adamant. If my name was on the cover then it would be my words inside that cover. *My* words and not a watered down version of the truth or the sycophantic rubbish that every journalist and self-styled political historian was writing in the aftermath of the glorious struggle for the survival of a continent. Nor would they be the words of my editor and publisher, who had never set foot on the shores of Africa. I told him all this a short time after my return; on a night when we'd both imbibed the best part of a bottle of Glen Morangie.

He had liked the chapter in which I'd praised Nelson Mandela's restraint since his release from Robben Island, and his subsequent wisdom of leadership after donning the mantle of ANC power. He had effectively prevented a bloodbath and I spelled that out very clearly.

What Neville *hadn't* liked was my referring to Mandela as an AK47-wielding terrorist before he'd been imprisoned, though I did continue that he'd returned from incarceration as a man of patience and vision. If

164

his prime objective had been to be the first black president of Southern Africa then he had gone about it in just the right way, for he had finally realised that ambition on the 28th April, 1992, when he won the first fair – and therefore righteous – election in the history of the country.

The things I'd learned with Tom Jackson had all found their way into the text – the good, the bad, and the indifferent.

As though attuned to my thoughts, Neville smiled engagingly over the rim of his glass and said, in that condescending tone he adopts most of the time, 'I might have been a trifle hasty when going over the initial proofs, old chap, but your powers of persuasion won the day.'

'Trifle hasty, my arse,' I snorted. 'You would have changed the whole sodden lot if you'd had your way.'

'Phillip, Phillip... what language,' he tut-tutted in mock horror. 'You've changed you know. Since your little trip to the African continent.'

'South Africa, Neville,' I almost hissed. 'It's still called South Africa. And what I saw there would change anyone.'

He proffered the bottle towards my glass but I placed a hand over it and shook my head. He shrugged, topped up his own and his voice changed.

'I know, Phillip, I know. I don't think I ever thanked you properly. For finding out about John, and keeping his name out of all that messy business. Poor boy.'

'Poor boy...' I growled. 'I did it for your sake, not his. You were his employer, and the magazine would have been blamed. If he wasn't blackmailing his lover then he was bloody *using* him. For God's sake...'

'No,' Neville shook his head slowly. 'No, he was only doing a story on Albrecht. He would never sleep with him. You see, it was John and *I* who were lovers.'

I wasn't really surprised. I'd always guessed in which direction Neville leaned, but I was surprised at his naivete. In some strange way I found it touching. No matter how hard-nosed someone is in business, their private life can be most revealing, for we all have our vulnerable spots and weak points.

Which reminded me – I had arranged to meet mine for dinner.

Marike and I (yes, we're still together) are renting a cute cottage in a tiny Suffolk village. She accepted a good offer from the BBC World Service, and after the book was finished I went back to documentary film work. I have plans for another book.

'Got to be going, Neville. Thanks for the drink,' I stood up and placed my glass on his desk. Then an idea came to me and I suppressed a grin. 'I'm meeting a friend for dinner nearby. How about joining us? It will take your mind off John and things.'

Neville allowed himself to be persuaded and we walked off down Oxford Street, collars turned up against the cold. As we drew near to the restaurant I couldn't help a small chuckle at what the next few minutes would bring.

You see, Neville knew nothing about Marike – I'd seen no reason to mention her, and they'd never met.

I couldn't wait to see his face when they did, for prejudice dies hard. Both on and off the African continent.

END